Life
Unexpected
Book Two

Someone
to Trust

Isaiah 26:3-4

Melanie D. Snitker

Someone to Trust
(Life Unexpected: Book 2)
© 2017 Melanie D. Snitker

Published by
Dallionz Media, LLC
P.O. Box 6821
Abilene, TX 79608

Cover: Blue Valley Author Services

Melanie D. Snitker
melaniedsnitker@gmail.com
www.melaniedsnitker.com

ISBN: 0-9975289-5-8
ISBN-13: 978-0-9975289-5-4

Blessed is the man who trusts in the Lord,
whose confidence is in him.
He will be like a tree planted by the water
that sends out its roots by the stream.
It does not fear when heat comes;
its leaves are always green.
It has no worries in a year of drought
and never fails to bear fruit.
Jeremiah 17:7-8

Chapter One

Brooke Pierce's Kia Rio barely made it through the busy intersection before it rolled to a stop at the curb. "Oh, come on!" She smacked the steering wheel with her palm, even though she knew it wouldn't make a difference. What was wrong with it this time? All it had to do was get her to the post office and back during her lunch break. Car trouble was the last thing she needed.

She tried to start it again. When that didn't work, she checked the time on her phone. She had forty minutes to make it back in time for her next appointment. She could walk to the Quintin Family Hair Salon by then, but most of her customers expected a hairdresser who looked decent and didn't smell of sweat. Considering it was August in Texas, she wouldn't be smelling too pretty by the time she got there.

Since her friends, Joel and Anna, were away on their honeymoon, it narrowed her list of potential rescuers down to Chess.

Brooke dialed his phone number, and he answered on the second ring.

"Hey, Brooke. Everything going okay?"

That deep voice made her pulse stutter like usual. She ignored her response to him, a process she should have patented after years of practice. "My car stalled and I can't get it started again."

"Where are you?"

Brooke craned her neck to see the street sign behind her. "I'm on the corner of Lockhart and Hyacinth."

"I'll be there in ten minutes." The connection went silent.

She released a sigh of relief. She could always count on her friends — her family — when something like this happened. That's what was so great about their group of four. They rallied together and helped each other in a way a lot of biological families didn't even do.

Someone knocked on the window and Brooke jumped. A guy she didn't know peered in at her. "Do you need help?"

Brooke shook her head but refused to roll down the window. She smiled. "No, thank you. Someone's on the way. I appreciate it though."

The guy returned her smile, waved, and jogged back to his vehicle. It'd been nice of him to stop.

She took another glimpse at the clock. If Chess said he'd be here in ten minutes, it meant he'd show up even sooner. Right on cue, his dark blue Ford F-150 pulled into the parking lot nearby. He got out and jogged to the passenger side where Brooke had rolled down the window.

Chess stooped and leaned in. "It won't start at

all?"

"Nope." To illustrate, Brooke turned the ignition and all they could hear was a faint clicking sound.

Chess frowned. "All right. I'll push and you steer into the parking lot where my truck is. I'll take you back to work and then call to have it towed." He gave the door a smack. "You ready?"

"Good to go."

With a firm nod, Chess moved to the back of the car. Brooke put it in neutral and easily guided it to a space next to his truck.

Chess ran his fingers through his sandy brown hair. He stood four inches taller than her and didn't seem the least bit bothered by having pushed the car. Not that it surprised her.

Chess held a hand out. "Let me have your key and I'll take care of everything."

Brooke didn't argue as she took the black key off her key ring. "Please bring me by when they're done so I can pay the bill." He reached for the key, but she held onto it. Their fingers touched, sending a jolt of electricity into her arm and jump-starting her heart rate again. She gave him a pointed look. She wouldn't put it past him to pay the bill for her since he knew she was trying to build up her savings account.

A corner of his mouth pulled to the side. "Fine."

"Thank you." She released the key, and he pocketed it. Despite the fact they were only friends, she could still feel where his hand had touched hers as though he'd left an imprint. The realization frustrated her. How many ages had she fought against this attraction? Sure, he all but saved her life when she and

Joel were eighteen. But he was as good as family.

Besides, Chess had never seen her as anything but a younger sister of sorts. She prayed, one day, her heart would finally grasp that truth and quit torturing her with dreams that would never be.

Chess put a hand on her back and steered her toward his truck. "Come on. I'll drive you back to work. You off at five today?"

"Five-thirty." She stepped up to the passenger seat and buckled in.

He walked around the front of the truck and got in behind the wheel. "I'll be there to pick you up. Why were you on this side of town?"

"We needed stamps."

Without saying another word, he drove the two blocks to the post office. "I'll wait here."

Brooke flashed him a grin before getting out and jogging to the main door. Thankfully, the line wasn't too long. She examined the stamp choices, made her decision, and rejoined Chess in minutes. "Thanks."

"You're welcome."

She thought about their newlywed friends. "I hope Joel and Anna are enjoying Hawaii."

Chess checked his rearview mirror and switched lanes. "Me, too. I still can't believe Joel took three weeks off from work. That's unheard of."

"He deserves the break. He works too hard. I'm glad they were able to take that much time off to start their lives together." The wistful tone in her voice surprised even her. "How's Epic doing without them?"

Anna's Great Pyrenees was staying with Chess while his owners were away. Unlike Brooke's tiny second-floor apartment that was completely unwelcoming to a monster-sized dog, Chess's house had a large backyard where Epic could run.

"He finally stopped sitting at the front door waiting for Anna yesterday. He's still moping a lot, though."

"Poor fella. He probably thinks she's gone for good. Don't tell her he's having a hard time or Anna will just feel bad."

Chess glanced at her. "Have you heard from either of them?"

She shook her head. "Not a peep since they let us know they got there safely." Joel and Anna got married a week ago in the park where they first met. "I imagine we'll hear from them soon, though."

They drove the rest of the way to the hair salon in silence. Brooke took in Chess's handsome profile as he maneuvered through Quintin. With a strong chin, wide shoulders, and determination in spades, he exuded confidence. She could count on a single hand the times he hadn't been in command of a situation. One of the many things that had drawn her to him — yet had also been the source of frequent disagreements. They could both be ridiculously stubborn. Even so, she respected him, counted on him.

She fought back a groan and leaned against her door. It was time to focus on something else. Anything else.

"Were you going anywhere this evening?"

Chess's words caught her off guard. "What?"

"Tonight. Did you need your car?"

"Oh. No. I have a date with Larry, but he's picking me up." Larry. The guy she *should* be thinking about, for crying out loud. She didn't miss the disapproving glance Chess shot her way as he pulled into a parking space in front of the salon.

"Someone new?"

"Second date."

Chess said nothing else, but his hazel eyes shifted to a shade of green, a sure sign there was more he wasn't voicing. He'd made his concerns clear about her frequent dating. Sure, she usually didn't see the same guy more than a handful of times. But when it was clear her date wasn't "the one," what was the point? She and Chess had had several arguments about that subject in the past.

Brooke knew he didn't approve, but it wasn't his business anyway, right? She forced down her irritation and gave him what she hoped was a normal smile. "Thanks for the ride, Chess. I owe you."

"Don't work too hard."

"I never do." She waved over her shoulder and pulled on the salon's door. A little bell announced her entrance as the combination of shampoo, conditioner, and hairspray welcomed her.

Brooke spotted her twelve forty-five appointment waiting for her. "Good afternoon, Mrs. Weston. If you'll come with me, we can get started. How are you today?"

The older lady stood and positioned her leather purse on her shoulder. She smiled brightly. "I'm wonderful, dear. How are you?"

Brooke learned long ago that it was best to keep her side of the conversation light. Being a hairdresser was a lot like being a bartender. You listened to your customers, gave them someone to talk to, and chatted about different hair products or styles. But you kept your problems to yourself. She shoved the myriad of concerns about her car into the corner of her mind where thoughts of Chess usually took up residence. "It's Friday. That always makes everything better."

Mrs. Weston laughed. "Isn't that the truth?"

Brooke led the way to a chair in front of a wide mirror and waited for her to take a seat. "So, what are we doing today?"

Mrs. Weston patted her hair. The silver strands cascaded to the middle of her back and shined under the salon lights. "Let's cut it to just above my shoulders. You know what? I'm tired of being gray, and I refuse to have my hair dyed a color no one believes is really mine." She laughed again, her eyes bright and almost mischievous. "What would it take to turn my hair purple?"

Brooke checked her customer's reflection in the mirror. Mrs. Weston appeared to be completely serious. Covering her surprise, Brooke's lips lifted in a smile. "Are you kidding? Purple would look great on you." She reached for a pick and gently began to work through the hair. "What gave you this brilliant idea?"

Mrs. Weston gave her a wink. "Honey, I only get to live once. I might as well make it colorful."

Chess watched as Brooke closed his truck's door. The sun hit her dark brown hair, bringing out the subtle red highlights. She disappeared into the salon.

Thinking about her date tonight brought a frown to his face. How many guys had she gone out with in the last few months alone? He certainly couldn't keep count. It wasn't healthy. And none of her relationships ever lasted long. He'd tried talking to her about it, but she got defensive.

All he wanted to do was sit and have a rational conversation about her relationship issues. It turned into an emotional argument he'd rather not repeat. Now he tried to mind his own business.

That didn't mean he stopped worrying — or caring — about her.

Brooke turned twenty-eight last month. She deserved to settle down with the right guy. But the men she usually dated... they weren't worth her time, much less her heart. Most of them deserved a good right cross — and there'd been a couple guys in the past where he'd been happy to oblige. He thought about one back in April who had cheated on Brooke because she wouldn't sleep with him. Yep, that guy received the good sock to the chin he deserved.

His smile faded as he backed out of the space and headed home again.

He had a lot of work left to do before he called it a day. They had a deadline for this software launch in two weeks, which meant they were all working overtime. Since he was on salary, that translated into evenings spent in front of the computer with not a lot to show for it.

Chess walked into his house where Epic greeted him, the dog's large tail sweeping back and forth in the air. Chess had to admit it was nice having someone to come home to. He'd shared this place with Joel and Brooke for a long time. When Anna joined the group earlier this year, she and Brooke decided to rent a house together.

Now that Joel moved into Anna's house after they got married, Chess had the place to himself. He still wasn't used to it. Brooke's old bedroom had a bed in it and Joel's held only Chess's desk and a bookshelf. It was nice having some office space, but he'd rather have his friends there instead.

He let Epic outside and then sat down at his computer. Three messenger screens blinked, waiting for a response. After pulling a granola bar out of a drawer, he set about answering the questions his long-distance co-workers had asked.

Sometimes this job frustrated him, but most of the time, he was grateful for it. Few employers out there would allow him to work from home three days a week. Mondays and Tuesdays, he made the nearly two-hour commute to the office on the east side of Dallas.

As a software engineer, being home allowed him to get more coding done. Not to mention, he could help his friends like he did Brooke today. So yeah, he had a lot to be thankful for.

Once he had everything back under control, he called to have Brooke's car towed to a mechanic they used. Sam promised he'd check it today. Since it was the end of the week, he probably wouldn't get to the repairs until Monday, which was what Chess had expected.

He was in front of the computer for the better part of the afternoon, glad to have an excuse to leave a little early to pick Brooke up again. When he parked in front of the salon, she was outside waiting for him.

She got settled in the passenger seat, and then Chess relayed the information about her vehicle.

Brooke frowned. "Thanks for having it towed. I just hope, whatever's wrong with it, it isn't something major."

"No sense in worrying about something that

hasn't happened yet. We'll deal with it as it comes." Chess waited for the light to change and pulled out of the parking lot. "Someday, though, you're going to have to get a new car."

She shot him an exasperated look. "Like I need to waste money on one. This car has served me well."

"Except when it doesn't."

Brooke shook her head. "Fine. Point taken. But it's going to have to keep limping along for a while."

"It'll all work out..." he started.

And they finished together "... it always does."

He smiled at her, glad to see the sparkle back in her eyes. "You need to stop anywhere before going home?"

Brooke said she didn't. Except for the country music playing on the radio, the rest of their short drive was silent.

Chess pulled into a parking spot below her apartment. "Be careful tonight."

Brooke offered him a mildly annoyed glare. "I will." She'd gone around the front of the truck when he rolled his window down and called her back over.

"Call me if you need anything, okay?"

She leaned down, her eyes on him. They were some of the deepest brown he'd ever seen. Most of the time, they were windows to her soul. With one hand on the door, she flashed him that smile he was sure could melt any man's heart. "Thanks, Chess."

She waved before walking toward the apartment building and the set of stairs that took her to the second floor. She had a tiny balcony decorated with a single rose bush.

Back when Anna and Brooke moved into a

rental together, Chess had bought the bush as a house-warming gift and planted it in the front yard. It'd grown from a scrawny thing into a healthy bush that regularly produced cream-colored blooms with pink edges. Brooke had been so sad about leaving it behind, that he'd dug it up again. He then planted it in a pot and made it possible for her to take it with her to her new apartment. The grateful smile she'd given him when he carried it up to the balcony for her had made the work worthwhile.

As she passed by the large rose bush, she touched one of the flowers with a single finger. She waved at him and went inside.

Man, he missed having her around all the time. It was bad enough when she'd moved out to rent the house with Anna.

He thought back to when he first saw Brooke in Dallas. She'd been a scrawny eighteen-year-old with a mouth that never stopped and the ability to push all his buttons. If it weren't for Joel standing in as the mediator, Chess doubted he and Brooke would've gotten along as well. Certainly not enough to turn their group of three into the family none of them had growing up.

She wasn't that annoying kid anymore. She'd grown into a beautiful woman with enough personality, empathy, and strength to get through anything. If someone had told him when he first met her that he'd become completely enamored with her, he would've called them crazy.

She'd make some lucky guy an amazing wife one day. The thought made his chest ache. Brooke deserved to find someone — to be happy.

A big part of Chess wanted that someone to be

him. His throat constricted. There were a lot of reasons why that couldn't happen, and he had no doubt he was making the right decision to guard his heart. By doing so, he was also keeping watch over hers.

Besides, Brooke had never seen him as more than a big brother and friend. When it came to opening up to people, she always ran to Joel. Now she dated one guy after the other, and Chess was left to take up the worried, chastising older brother position. Which only seemed to annoy her more and made Chess feel even less connected to her than before.

It didn't matter, they were friends, a role assigned to them for far too long to change. It was better that way. Chess put the pickup in reverse harder than he needed to and headed back home. He had work to do and the last thing he needed was to think about Brooke and her date tonight.

Chapter Two

Pings from Chess's cell phone announced messages before he even sat down at his desk. He spent several minutes dealing with them and then took a moment to check social media. A notification at the top said he had a friend request. Not completely uncommon though most of his social media contacts were co-workers.

He clicked on it so he could see the name.

Nathan Kirkpatrick.

At first, it meant little. He didn't know any Kirkpatricks, and the only Nathan he'd known he hadn't seen since he was nine. He clicked on the profile picture. A photo of Jackie Chan breaking a board with his hands didn't exactly help Chess figure out who the guy was.

It was the location that drew his attention. Homestead, Florida. He scanned the rest of the information and stopped when he saw that Nathan had also lived in Dallas, Texas.

Chess froze. Adrenaline surged while his hands

grew cold.

No way. Was Nathan Kirkpatrick truly his long-lost brother? Surely not. It had to be a coincidence.

Chess moved to accept Nathan Kirkpatrick's friend request several times before stopping himself. Just because the first name and the location matched, it didn't mean this was the Nathan he used to know. He pictured his tow-headed little brother. Nathan was four and relied on Chess for everything. Chess still remembered the fear and confusion in Nathan's eyes the last time Chess saw him.

Feelings of incompetence pounded his chest. He'd beaten himself up for not knowing what happened to his little brother and not being there to take care of him. It was his responsibility to keep the two of them together, and he'd failed miserably.

Uncertain, Chess decided to think about the friend request and absently cooked a frozen dinner in the microwave. If Brooke saw what he was eating, she'd have chided him for it.

When the three of them lived together, they rarely ate frozen food. Brooke knew how to cook and enjoyed it. Which meant he and Joel had become spoiled. His thoughts flew back to the friend request again. After all these years, he'd never told Joel or Brooke about Nathan. He hadn't talked about his past much at all. And while Brooke and Joel were curious in the beginning, Chess couldn't remember the last time the topic had come up.

His stomach clenched, and he suddenly didn't feel like eating the Salisbury steak.

Maybe it was time to talk to his friends about Nathan. Joel might understand why he never spoke of him. But would Brooke? She used to ask him about his past all the time and he'd avoided answering her questions. Would finding out how much he'd kept from her put yet more distance between them?

He swallowed down his frustration. There was no point in worrying about it now. Especially when he didn't know for sure this was even the Nathan he thought it might be.

Chess forced himself to take a bite of his dinner when his phone rang. He looked at the caller ID and saw it was Joel. He answered, forcing a smile on his face he hoped would bleed into his voice. "Hey! How's married life treating you?"

"Amazing. You should try it yourself sometime."

Yeah, that's not happening. He could hear a combination of birds and people's voices in the background. "Sounds busy there."

"We're checking out one of the beaches. It would seem it's a popular choice. We'll probably ask at the hotel tomorrow and see if there's another that's not quite as crowded." There was a muffled sound before Joel spoke again. "Anastasia's wondering how Epic's doing."

Chess glanced at the time. He'd forgotten Hawaii was five hours behind Texas. It was early afternoon there. Chess moved his foot and nudged Epic. The poor guy never left Chess's side. "He's right here and doing fine. He's eating well, and I've taken him to the park twice this week. I can tell he misses you guys, though."

"We miss him, too. I think he'd love running in the surf here." Joel laughed. "What are you and Brooke up to this week?"

"Oh, you know. Work and more work." He

told his friend about Brooke's car. "She's going on another date tonight."

"She mentioned it to Anastasia when they talked a few minutes ago." He paused. "I guess this guy moved here from Colorado or something like that."

Chess shook his head. "Where does she meet all these guys when she works at a salon? It's mostly women who go in there."

"Yes. Mothers and grandmothers who have sons or grandsons they try to set up." Joel's voice was laced with amusement. "Is this older brother talking? Or jealousy?"

Only a handful of times in the past had Joel insinuated Chess might have feelings for Brooke. He hadn't appreciated it then, and he didn't now, either. He frowned. "Don't even start, man."

"All right. My point is, when you criticize her dates, you're walking a fine line. And Brooke is sensitive about it. Don't push her, Chess."

Joel was right. Chess cared about Brooke — way more than he should. And if she knew he was here talking about her date, she'd be furious. "I'll stay out of it. Don't worry."

"We told Brooke she can use Anastasia's car while hers is in the shop."

"That'll be great. I'll take her to go pick it up tomorrow." Since he had to drive into Dallas Monday and Tuesday, he wouldn't be there to give Brooke a ride. Although, if he'd needed to, he'd have taken the days off. When was the last time he hung out with just Brooke? He couldn't even remember.

"All I ask is that you two try not to kill each other while we're gone." Apparently, Joel was thinking along the same lines.

"Funny. I think we'll survive. You guys have fun. And try to convince Anna that Epic is fine."

Joel chuckled at that. "Will do. We'll call again in a few days."

They said their goodbyes. Chess poked the now-cold meal with his fork and wrinkled his nose. He stood and Epic jumped to his feet, following Chess into the kitchen. "I think you'll enjoy this more than I will."

He set the plate on the floor for Epic to gobble down and poured himself a bowl of cereal. He took that back to his computer and sat again to stare at the friend request.

Chess finally sent a short private message asking, *"Who is this?"*

Chess stared at the screen as it showed the other person read his message and was typing a response. His cereal forgotten, Chess leaned forward in nervous anticipation.

"I'm searching for a Chester Summers from the Dallas/Fort Worth area."

Chess's fingers stilled and the words on the screen blurred before becoming clear again. He'd searched for his baby brother for years before giving up. But why hadn't Nathan sought Chess out before now? And why the different last name?

Chess inhaled and typed out a response.

"I'm originally from Dallas. Who are you?"

A response came quickly this time.

"I'm searching for my brother. We were separated as kids. When I was young, a couple adopted me, and I took their last name of Kirkpatrick. A year or two later, we moved to Florida. My last name was Summers."

Chess's chest burned, a melting pot of

emotions. Relief that Nathan was alive mixed with disbelief, and all of that coated in a layer of apprehension. He realized, from this moment on, his life would never be the same. He stared at the computer screen. His hands felt disconnected from his body as he typed several things, only going back to erase them afterwards.

Holding his breath, he typed out a response and hit enter before he changed his mind.

"I looked for you for most of my life. I had no idea your last name had been changed."

A few minutes went by.

"I searched for you because I have to know. What happened? Did you send me away?"

The words took several moments to penetrate Chess's brain. *"It wasn't like that. I never wanted you to leave. You were the only younger child in our foster home. It was packed, and I was told they moved you somewhere else. I didn't want them to."*

That was a gross understatement. His foster father had had to hold him back as the case worker picked up Nathan and carried him out the front door. Chess squeezed his eyes shut to block out the memory of Nathan crying, his arms reaching for his big brother. Another ping and he opened them again.

"They told me you didn't want to go with me."

Chess shook his head, trying to comprehend what Nathan was saying. If that was true, had he grown up thinking Chess didn't care about him? The possibility made him sick. What kind of people would do such a thing? *"No one would tell me where you were or what happened to you."*

When Nathan said nothing else, Chess accepted the friend request that had been waiting for a response.

Every fear and insecurity he had about Nathan came crashing down on him. He'd spent most of his life trying to convince himself he'd done everything he could to be reunited with his brother. But all of that didn't matter if Nathan thought Chess hadn't wanted him in the first place. Maybe, if they talked, they'd figure out the truth between them.

Brooke tried to tune out the sound of her neighbors arguing. They were in the apartment right below hers. In the month she'd lived there, this was the third time they'd had a dispute complete with screaming, name calling, and slamming of doors. They were at it half the night until one of them finally left the building and all fell quiet. Apparently, they were ready for round two.

She wasn't a fan of living here. She missed having a yard, not to mention peace and quiet. Most of all, though, she missed having a roommate.

Silly, maybe. But this was the first time in her life she'd lived on her own. She'd left foster care with Joel, then it was the two of them plus Chess. Later, it was her and Anna.

Brooke was an independent woman now. She moved out of the rental house so that Joel could move in after he and Anna got married. Brooke ought to be happy she had sole possession of the remote control. She didn't have to keep reminding one guy or another to put his plate in the kitchen or sweep whiskers off the bathroom counter when he'd finished shaving. She didn't have to coordinate with Anna on who got to shower first in the morning.

During the week when she was working, she could almost convince herself all of that was true. But Saturday afternoons and Sundays, she'd trade it all to not be alone in her apartment.

She hadn't heard from Larry since their date last night. Not that their evening had been overly fantastic. They went out to dinner and then stopped for ice cream afterwards. The dish of chocolate and strawberry was definitely the highlight. Their awkward kiss when he took her back home didn't exactly have her counting down until the next date. How sad was that?

Her phone chimed with a text. She immediately smiled when she saw it was from Chess.

"I thought I'd come by and take you to get Anna's car. Joel told me where an extra key is in the house. Are you busy?"

Not unless feeling sorry for herself counted. *"Nope, I'm free. I'll be waiting outside."*

She sat down on the steps and kept busy with a game on her phone until Chess's truck pulled up. Once seated inside, she looked over and smiled. "I appreciate this."

"No problem. I've got a deadline in two weeks so I'll be late getting home Monday and Tuesday. I'm glad you'll have Anna's car that way you're not stranded." He maneuvered the truck out of the parking lot.

"I'll come by at lunch and after work to let Epic outside if you want me to."

His eyes shifted to hers and he grinned. "That'd be great, thank you."

"Sure." She focused on her phone as she added reminders to her calendar for the next couple of days.

They all had exchanged keys to each other's places. It was mostly for emergencies, but they came in handy for situations like these as well.

Once they got to Anna and Joel's house, it was easy to find the spare keys to the car parked in the driveway. This was the house she'd rented with Anna and she missed it. But it made more sense for the newlyweds to move in until they found a house they wanted to buy.

Minutes later, she was ready to slide into Anna's car and head back to her apartment. She hesitated. Normally, the whole gang would get together for dinner tonight or tomorrow. Last weekend was the wedding, and it made sense she and Chess did nothing. But this weekend, it would've been nice to get together and see a movie or something.

Chess's eyes narrowed as he watched her. "Is something wrong?"

What was she supposed to say? That she'd become so co-dependent the thought of spending a weekend alone made her want to cry? Nope, she wouldn't do that.

"I'm just tired. My neighbors downstairs argued off and on all last night."

"You need to bang on your floor with a broom handle every time they yell at each other."

"Sure. Then I can turn into Mr. Heckles from *Friends*." They both chuckled.

"Well, it'd serve them right." He grinned. "I'll call you next week as soon as I hear from the mechanic."

Brooke forced a smile. "Sounds good. Have a great weekend, Chess."

"You, too." He gave her a little wave and got

into his truck.

With a slow sigh that matched the sad song on the radio, Brooke headed home again. It would be a long few days.

Chapter Three

Brooke observed the Wednesday lunch crowd at her favorite Mexican food restaurant. Chess had picked her up at Anna's house to go to lunch and then swing by and retrieve her car from the mechanic. She was more than ready to have her own vehicle back again.

Chess set a plate down in front of Brooke before sliding into the booth opposite her. She picked up her fork and twirled the melted cheese around it, the tangy smell of the red sauce filling her nostrils. The moment the food touched her tongue, her eyes drifted closed. The cheese and sauce were a perfect combination. "No one makes enchiladas like Mr. Torres."

"They are good." Chess took a bite of his own lunch. He'd gone with beef enchiladas instead of cheese. "I don't think they're better than yours, though. I like how they give you enough food here, not like that place across town."

Brooke flashed him a happy smile. Both Chess and Joel had repeatedly mentioned how much they enjoyed her cooking. Even when they didn't say it, the speed at which they put it away spoke volumes. She observed the three enchiladas, refried beans, rice, and a small pile of lettuce topped with tomato on her plate. "There's no way I'll be able to eat all of this." She knew, though, that Chess would have no problem cleaning his plate.

They ate in comfortable silence for a few minutes until Chess spoke from his side of the table. "How's work going today?"

She shrugged. "It's fine."

That got his attention. His eyes narrowed. "What's wrong?"

Brooke studied the busy dining area. She recognized none of the salon's regulars, but that didn't mean others who frequented the business weren't there. She didn't want to be overheard and leaned forward, her voice lowered. "We get many people in who like to gossip. I usually let it roll off my back but sometimes…" Today, they'd had two different people come in and complain about the other. It was exhausting, especially when Brooke hated to hear either of them bashed. She told Chess as much.

Chess took a swig of his soda. "I remember when you used to find all the odd things your customers said to be funny. Do you not like your job anymore?"

"It's okay." Brooke shrugged. He was right. She used to come home with stories of the funny things the ladies said and took it all in stride. And usually she was fine. She didn't mind hearing about everyone else's troubles, their family, their vacations. But then there were days like today. Chess was studying her, obviously not buying it. "It's nearby. I can't complain about that. And the job was a huge factor in getting me to where I am now." It'd taught her a lot about responsibility, given her financial freedom, and helped her to contribute to their family, which Chess had mostly carried for the first year or so.

It made her feel independent back then. But now, she was tiring of the mundane routine. She'd never imagined doing this for so long. At the least, she'd expected to be in a long-term relationship by now, for crying out loud.

He put his fork down. "You don't have to stay there. If there's something else you want to pursue, we can make that happen. You could even go back to school."

That was about the last thing she'd expected Chess to say. She blinked at him.

Apparently, he took her pause as a sign something was wrong. "What?"

Brooke shook her head. "It's sad because I don't even know what I'd go back to school for."

"Don't you have vacation saved up? Maybe you need to use it. Get away from the salon for a while."

Brooke shrugged. "I don't simply need a break. I guess I always thought my job would be temporary until…" Heat started at the base of her neck and traveled to her face. This was something she could probably talk to Joel about. Maybe Anna. But Chess? She had his full attention, though, and she knew he wouldn't let it go now. "I only wanted to work until I got married and started a family. Then I hoped to be at home with my kids. I guess I always thought working at the salon would be a short-term gig." Now her face was flaming, and she wished they weren't sitting so close to a window that highlighted the blush. Too bad they weren't over there in the shadows on the other side of the room.

When she and Joel first met Chess, he had a full-time job. It wasn't anything flashy and often involved shift work, but he could support the two of them while they got themselves together and found jobs of their own. That last part was something he insisted they do, too. He'd told them it taught responsibility and would be the first step toward providing for themselves. In fact, Chess had made that point many times the first six months until Brooke had tired of hearing it.

But he'd been right. By the end of that first year, they were back on their feet. Joel and Brooke expected Chess to ask them to leave and find their own place to live. He never did and slowly the relationships became less like tenants and more like family.

Chess had put such an emphasis on the importance of working, what did he think of her admitting she wanted to stay home when she had kids? Did he consider her lack of dedication to her job a weakness? She kept her eyes on the window and then the bubbles of carbonation rising in her glass.

Chess reached across the table and lightly tapped her hand. "There's nothing wrong with that, Brooke. I think we all wish we'd grown up in households where we came home from school to a parent waiting for us with snacks, hugs, and help with homework." His voice sounded husky, and he cleared his throat. "You'll be an amazing mom one day."

His words brought tears to her eyes. She fought to blink them away.

She got the sense he might have said more if it

hadn't been for their surroundings. Brooke was just as happy to end the conversation there herself. The last thing she wanted to do was cry in front of him, which is exactly what his support made her want to do. She swallowed and then forced a smile. "Don't mind me. You know I get emotional when I have to pay to get my car out of jail."

Whether Chess believed her or chose to let the moment pass, Brooke wasn't sure. But she appreciated he accepted the change in topic.

"If you need a loan, let me know."

"I should be good, but thanks." Brooke offered another smile and then went back to her lunch.

A half hour later, they arrived at the auto body shop. Brooke had enough money to pay for the work, but it made a dent in her savings. She wasn't overly thrilled with that, but she needed her vehicle to get around so it had to be done. The damage could have been a lot worse.

She was standing outside her car with Chess. "Thanks again for lunch and for arranging everything with my car. I appreciate it."

Chess gave a short nod. "You're welcome. Don't let work get to you this afternoon, okay? Are you going anywhere tonight?"

Brooke shook her head while simultaneously wishing she could go over to Chess's house. "No. I have another date with Larry tomorrow night, though."

Something passed over Chess's face and was gone again before Brooke could fully interpret it. "Text me when you get home tonight and tomorrow, okay? Maybe we can eat dinner together Friday night."

She grinned. "I will, and that sounds great. See

you later, yeah?"

"Yeah."

Brooke turned the key in the ignition, thankful when the engine started. She backed out of the parking space and made her way through the parking lot. Chess remained where she left him until he was no longer in sight.

Could she actually make a change in her career now? It might take forever for her Prince Charming to finally show up. Correction: She'd driven away from him. But she could spend the rest of her life waiting for him to see her as more than an annoying little sister he had to keep tabs on.

Annoyance boiled until she thought it would spill over. She'd already tortured herself for a decade. Why did she allow herself to keep her life in limbo like this?

Brooke gripped the arms of the passenger seat the moment Larry pulled into The Broken Dawn's parking lot Thursday night. She didn't drink and had no personal experience with it or any other bar. But she'd heard this one had a reputation for being busy and a little rough. "Why are we here? I thought we were going to the drive-in to see a movie?"

Larry put his truck in park and turned off the engine. "A friend of mine asked if I'd meet him here for a few minutes first." He jumped down and went around to open her door. "You're welcome to wait out here if you want to." His expression was guarded, and she wasn't sure whether he wanted her to stay or go with him.

All kinds of warning bells were going off and Brooke wanted to protest. But Larry was walking toward the building. It was late, the sun was setting fast, and she wasn't sure sitting outside in a dark parking lot was any safer. She picked up the pace and hurried after him.

The moment she stepped inside, the combination of alcohol, greasy food, and faint cigarette smoke assaulted her senses. Brooke took in the surrounding scene, thankful the bar limited smoking to one section. But from the smell of it, that didn't mean the smoke adhered to the rules. She resisted the urge to wrinkle her nose against the combination.

More than anything else, it was the sheer noise of all the people that gave Brooke an instant headache. With loud music playing and people talking over each other, how did anyone hold a conversation?

Larry didn't even check behind him to make sure Brooke was following. Instead, he charged ahead, parting groups of people until he'd led the way to the game area. There were two pool tables, a variety of game consoles along one wall, and several dartboards. Gobs of people were everywhere. Brooke fought against the waves of claustrophobia.

They approached a group of guys on the other side of a pool table. The moment they recognized Larry, there were whoops and high fives. "Hey, what's up?" He took a mug of beer someone offered him and chugged half of it down.

All Brooke could do was stare. She didn't even try to parse out what each person was saying. She only wanted Larry to say hi so they could be on their way.

One of the guys playing pool noticed Brooke and frowned. He gave Larry a pointed look. Brooke could've sworn Larry cringed. He tipped his head toward her. "Hey, all. This is my girl. We were going to go see a movie tonight but thought we'd stop by for a while."

His girl? He wasn't even going to tell them her name? And from what she could see, the others couldn't care less Larry had brought her along. If Brooke hadn't had enough of this experience already, that solidified her impression. She turned to Larry and raised her voice enough to be heard over all the noise. "Hey, I'd like to get going. It's getting late."

He barely glanced at her, took a pool cue from one of the other guys, and added some blue chalk to the tip. "We'll go see a movie another night. Do you play pool?"

"No." Brooke planted her hands on her hips. She was tired after not sleeping much last night and being on her feet all day. Then they'd waited forever for a table at one of the local restaurants and it took forty minutes to get their food. Not going to see the movie was fine with her. But if that were the case, she wanted to call it a night. "Please take me home, Larry? I'm not feeling well."

Larry kept his eyes on the pool table. "In a while. Why don't you go get a drink while I play this game?"

Nice to know I'm invisible. Brooke crossed her arms in front of her. She wasn't sure if she felt more like crying or screaming. Well, she wasn't getting something to drink here. She took several steps back and tried to feign interest in the game.

Larry downed two mugs of beer that Brooke counted as the game continued. She had no idea a game of pool could last so blasted long. Finally, he took the last shot. As he did, she stepped away from the wall. He hollered, lifting his hands and pool stick into the air. Apparently, he'd won.

"Can we leave now, please?"

Larry turned to face her and stumbled forward. The pool stick he still held came down and around, striking Brooke across her left cheekbone.

She gasped as the skin stung and grew warm. With one hand on her face, she watched in disbelief as the rest of the guys chortled.

Larry seemed shocked. "I didn't mean to." He looked at his so-called friends who were still cackling over the incident and straightened his spine. "You shouldn't sneak up on your man like that. Go ask for some ice up at the bar. I'm going to play another game, and then I'll take you home."

His lack of concern hit her harder than the stick had. None of his friends even gave her a second thought. Fighting back tears of infuriation and humiliation, she whirled and pushed her way through the crowd to the door.

How had she been this stupid? Sure, Larry wasn't the greatest guy around. And she'd pretty much decided to call an end to their dating after dinner, anyway. But how could she not know he was such a world class jerk? Why did she keep finding these guys?

What's wrong with me?

Once that first tear escaped, it was like the tip of a tidal wave. More raced each other down her face. She leaned against the brick wall, half illuminated by the bright lights at the front of the bar, and half hidden in the darkness. She drew in a ragged breath, sank to the concrete beneath her, and dug the cell phone out of her bag.

Chapter Four

Chess rolled his head to relieve the stiffness in his neck causing Epic to shift positions at his feet. Chess glanced at the time. Brooke was probably out on her date with Larry about now. She'd texted him when she got home from work, and he asked her to text him again when Larry took her home no matter how late it was. There was no way he was going to bed until he knew she'd returned safely.

He certainly had plenty of work to keep him busy until then. He'd be glad when he finished this project and they could push the new software out to their customers. There would always be something else on the horizon, but usually it meant a week or two of normalcy before the next one kicked in.

Even still, he had to force his attention back on his work and not think too hard about whether Brooke was doing okay or not. He opened private messaging and read through the conversation he and Nathan had over the last few days. Nathan apologized for not being online much and when they chatted, it was mostly about jobs and the cities where they lived. Nothing much more personal than that. Chess was tempted to write out his side of what happened, but something kept stopping him. If Nathan didn't want to talk about it yet, Chess would wait. He didn't want to risk losing this connection because he was getting impatient.

Not for the first time, Brooke came to mind. There was something off about her at lunch the other day. He'd originally thought it had to do with work, but he had a feeling there was another factor in play. If Joel were here, Chess would mention it to him. And then, either Joel or Anna might bring it up with Brooke. Assuming she hadn't spoken to them.

But Chess and Brooke? They tried to steer clear of discussions that got too personal or emotional. He knew it was because he had made a point of distancing himself from them back in the beginning.

Chess remembered how Brooke, especially, would ask him about his past and how he entered the foster care system and later got a place of his own. He'd told them about working his way to an associate's degree in computer programming and how he'd lucked into an internship that eventually led to the job he had now. But about what happened prior to that? Chess never said a word.

Brooke had been inquisitive back then. He'd had to tell her to quit asking him and to mind her own business. He could still picture the flash of pain in her eyes. In true Brooke fashion, she'd moved on from that. She never asked him about his past again.

When Chess thought about how much closer she was to Joel, his heart ached. Truthfully? He was a little jealous of it. In hindsight, he regretted not opening himself up to Brooke more. But after everything with his biological family…

When his phone rang a few minutes later, he lifted it from the desk. The moment he saw Brooke's name on the caller ID, his chest tightened. "Hey, Brooke." Why was she calling instead of simply texting? Had she locked herself out of the apartment? She'd brought over a spare key just in case that happened. Chess stood, prepared to retrieve it from a drawer in the kitchen.

A muffled sniff stopped him dead in his tracks. "What's wrong?"

"I need you to come pick me up. Please."

If Chess suspected she was crying before, he was certain of it now. Brooke was trying to hide the fact, but he detected the wobble in her voice. "Absolutely. Where are you?" He shoved his keys into a pocket and automatically tapped a hand to the forty-five he wore concealed at his hip.

"The Broken Dawn."

Chess faltered in his trek to the front door. A bar? What was she doing there? She'd never been one to drink alcohol or go to a place like that before. But now wasn't the time to question her about anything. Whatever happened, Larry must have left her stranded. "I'll be there in five minutes."

"Thanks, Chess." She ended the call.

He would have preferred to keep her on the line until he arrived.

It wasn't hard to spot her when he pulled up. She was sitting on the ground, her back to the brick outer wall of the bar. Bright lights outside kept the place well-lit, and for that he was grateful. The moment she saw him, she stood and hurried to the passenger side. She pulled the door open, the overhead light illuminating the cab.

Brooke buckled her seatbelt as the interior light faded, shadowing her expression. She rested her elbow on the door and kept her profile to him.

Chess wanted to ask her for details with everything he had in him, but he'd learned long ago that Brooke would share when she was good and ready. Instead, he drove her home.

With a hand on her lower back, he escorted her up the steps to her apartment and waited for her to unlock the door. Chess followed her in and secured the door behind them. They walked into the living room. When Brooke turned to face him, his gaze zeroed in on the purple bruise forming on her right cheekbone.

He took three long strides in her direction until he was close enough to touch the skin around the mark with a finger. Rage boiled inside and it took everything Chess had to keep his voice at a normal level. "Did Larry do this? I swear, I'll hunt him down…"

"It wasn't on purpose." Brooke rubbed her forehead and took a steadying breath. "He was drunk and goofing off. He turned and hit me with a pool cue."

That did little to take away the anger Chess was swimming in right now. So, what, the guy got drunk. He also hit his date by accident and left her in front of a bar at eleven o'clock at night. That didn't sit well with him.

Brooke finally moved to the couch and sank into the cushions. She wrapped her arms around her torso, and her silence was as alarming as the bruise on her face.

Chess sat down next to her, more than willing to wait her out. A tear made it halfway down Brooke's cheek before she swiped it away. The sight broke Chess's heart. This is when Joel or Anna would sit down with her and find out what happened. Then Chess would fix the problem. That's what he did; he was the problem solver. He had every intention of locating Larry and conducting a lesson or two on how to be a gentleman.

Trying to maneuver his way through a woman's emotions had never been his strong point. But he had the urge to pull her into his arms and try to comfort her somehow. He couldn't even remember the last time he gave Brooke a hug. Seeing as she was one of the most important people in Chess's life, the realization hit him like a punch to the stomach. He should hold her, or ask if there was someone she wanted to talk to. Or even better, he should be pummeling Larry right now. Why was he hesitating?

There were few times in his adult life he felt this helpless, and he despised it.

Brooke wiped away another tear. Why did she have to cry in front of Chess? She could sense his discomfort, but the tears refused to disappear and so here she was, a complete mess as usual. She'd gone through one of the most embarrassing nights in a long, long time. Something she'd rather no one find out about, most of all Chess.

He wasn't going anywhere though. She might as well spill it. Then maybe she could curl up on the couch and have a good, ugly cry by herself.

Brooke sat up straight and brushed some hair out of her face. In doing so, she touched the sore spot and winced, the pain in her cheek a cruel reminder of the horrible night she'd had.

"I know I screwed up. He said it would be one game and then he'd take me home. I should've called a cab when we first got to the bar instead of waiting for him. I don't know what—"

Chess's voice interrupted. "This is not your fault. Larry's no better than a..." He stopped with a growl, swallowing back what he'd been about to say. He clenched his fist in aggravation. "I'd like to get a hold of him right now."

Brooke crossed her arms in front of her, suddenly cold. "What's the point? He's probably passed out in an alley somewhere." She'd text him and tell him they were done. His grandmother came to the salon frequently. Ugh, hopefully Larry would keep his failed relationship to himself. She sure didn't need everyone gossiping about it. "I wish I hadn't even gone inside. But it was getting dark, and I figured it was better than sitting in the truck in the parking lot by myself."

Chess stood from the couch and retrieved the afghan draped over a nearby chair. He carefully spread it out over her lap before he disappeared into the kitchen. Brooke heard him rummaging in the freezer. Moments later, he returned with ice wrapped in a towel and sat down on the coffee table facing her, his knees on either side of hers. He reached over and held the cooling towel to her cheek.

His thoughtfulness nearly brought another round of tears. She pulled the soft edge of the afghan up to her chest and welcomed the warmth it provided. Then she reached up to cover his hand with her own. The contact resulted in tingles dancing across the surface of her skin. He kept his hand there a moment before withdrawing and leaving her to hold the ice. He moved to sit next to her on the couch again.

Brooke had prepared for the lecture she was sure Chess would give her. Instead, he was showing nothing but concern and that warmed her more than the blanket. What she needed, though, was for someone who cared to hold her. Every inch of her needed Chess to gather her into his arms and make her feel safe. Did she dare? She closed her eyes and leaned against him. She hadn't known what to expect, but when he lifted his arm and placed it around her shoulders, drawing her closer to him, a contented sigh escaped her lips.

"Thanks, Chess. For picking me up, for the ice, for the blanket." She paused. "For being here."

He didn't respond for several heartbeats. "You're welcome. I'm sorry this happened to you."

All she could do was shrug. She wanted to stay there in his arms indefinitely, but that was probably a terrible idea. The way her heart was pounding confirmed that fact. This would only make stepping back and going to their normal relationship tomorrow that much harder. "I'm okay." She made herself sit up straight again. "I think I want to take a shower to get the cigarette smoke off me and go to bed."

The concern in his eyes shifted to uncertainty. "Are you sure? I can stay for a while if you want."

Her heart begged her to say yes, but she shook her head. "Really, I'm fine. I need some rest and to pretend like tonight didn't happen." Well, except for how sweet he'd been. It was almost worth dealing with Larry earlier. Brooke stood then and Chess followed suit.

"You'll call if you need anything?"

She nodded.

"Promise?"

"I promise." She brought the ice pack down but kept it in her hand.

They walked to the front door together. Chess opened it but turned to Brooke again. He took her hand in his and gently raised it, along with the ice, back up to her face. "Keep it on there for a little while longer. It'll keep the swelling down." His hand lingered on hers for a moment before he pivoted and walked through the door. "Make sure you lock this behind me."

Brooke gave him what she hoped was a reassuring smile and waved before doing exactly as he'd asked. She leaned against it and let her eyes drift shut. She could still smell the spice from Chess's aftershave and feel the warmth of his arms around her.

Her heart pounded, and she released a slow breath. "Thank you, Lord, for protecting me. For keeping me safe. And for sending Chess to help me." She let her head fall back against the door several times. "Please help me to let go of these feelings I have for him. I think part of me has been hoping that one day, he'll see me differently. But I can't keep…" Tears clogged her throat.

With a frustrated shake of her head, she pushed away from the door. It was time to take a shower and try to wash away the memories of today.

Chapter Five

All day Friday, Chess couldn't get the sight of Brooke and the mark on her face out of his head. He could still feel her in his arms, vulnerable and yet strong at the same time. Holding her had probably been a mistake. But she'd needed someone and for once, it was him. It'd felt good to be there for her.

He despised what happened to her though. He still seethed about what Larry had done. If he knew where to find the guy... Brooke had wanted him to go last night, but he'd spent then and all day worrying about her and wondering if she was doing okay.

The day dragged until that evening when Chess ushered Brooke into his house for dinner like they'd arranged earlier in the week. She insisted on bringing the food, and he didn't argue with her since he'd mostly eaten frozen dinners or out of cans all week.

Thankfully the bruise didn't appear nearly as bad as he'd thought it would. It was visible, but it could've been much worse. The pool cue had been a mere inch or two away from giving her a black eye as well. Brooke insisted it didn't hurt much and handed him the bags of food she'd brought with her.

"What are we having?"

She tossed him an amused smile. "You'll see in a minute."

Chess chuckled as he set the bags on the kitchen counter. Brooke may be a lot of things, but boring wasn't one of them. In fact, he'd have to say she was one of the most unpredictable elements in his life. Something that used to drive him crazy in that first year after she and Joel moved into his tiny apartment. But now he welcomed it. Well, except for the part about having to pick her up from a bar. He could do without that.

Had she spoken to Larry again? Had the guy at least apologized for getting drunk and not making sure she got home again safely?

Epic lifted his head against Brooke's hand, reminding her that he was there and needed an ear scratch or two. She knelt and obliged. "I'll bet you're anxious to have Anna back, aren't you, boy? Is this guy over here boring you?"

"Ha-ha, funny." Chess lifted an eyebrow at her. "It just so happens we get along great, thank you very much."

Brooke kissed the top of Epic's head and stood again. "Everything's hot and ready to eat."

Chess got plates and silverware out as Brooke unpacked the bags and took it to the dining room table. He sat down and observed the fare. Fried chicken, mashed potatoes, gravy, and corn on the cob. His favorite. He lifted his gaze to meet hers across the table.

Her cheeks turned pink, and she shrugged as if the meal were no big deal. "I wanted to thank you for what you did last night. I appreciate it. Besides, I haven't made fried chicken in forever."

"Well, thanking me wasn't necessary, but I'm not turning down a feast like this. Thank you."

She grinned.

Chess took a bite of fried chicken. Butter and cornmeal combined with the right amount of garlic. Perfect. He noticed Brooke hesitated before eating her own food. She'd always been one to pray before a meal, even if it was silently. It was one of the few things they'd disagreed about since day one. She and Joel were Christians. But Chess... Well, he wasn't even sure God existed. And if He did, He'd certainly never cared one bit about what happened in Chess's life. Either way, Chess wasn't interested.

He shook off the thoughts and focused on his food. Epic sat on the other side of the room, his eyes following their every move.

Brooke tilted her head toward the dog. "Does he always do that?"

"I might give him more scraps than Anna does. But who's counting?"

Brooke giggled. "I'm thinking Epic is."

Chess raised a mischievous eyebrow. "Epic and I have agreed to not say a thing when Joel and Anna get back." He took a bite of his corn and winked at Epic.

"You're something else." She pointed a thumb toward the kitchen. "I noticed the empty can of soup on the counter. Is that what you had for lunch?"

He looked at her, and they both smiled. "It is. Though not anywhere near as good as what you used to make, though."

She laughed. "What? You didn't cook up

some rice, chop a few carrots, and serve it on a platter?"

He remembered well how, not long after she and Joel moved into his apartment, food was a little thin. Brooke somehow took a can of soup and turned it into a meal. Even now, opening a can of soup brought a wave of nostalgia. "I dumped it into a bowl, nuked it in the microwave, and ate it with a spoon. But it always makes me think of those early days. That soup tasted as good as steak at the time."

"Yeah, it did. We've come a long way since then."

Chess enjoyed the sound of her laughter until his gaze rested on her bruise and he sobered. They ate in comfortable silence. When they'd finished, Brooke got up to clear the table, but Chess stopped her. "I was wondering if I could talk to you about something."

"Sure."

"Let's go sit down."

Brooke took a seat on the couch and Chess joined her, angling his body to face her. She watched him expectantly. He cleared his throat. "Did I mess things up when you and Joel first came to stay with me?"

Her eyes narrowed. "What are you talking about?"

Chess rubbed his chin with one hand. "You used to ask me all the time how I ended up in foster care or question me about my family. I pretty much told you to leave me alone back then." He paused. "Joel and I get along well. You and Joel have a special bond. But I think I messed that up between us, didn't I?"

Brooke shrugged. "I wouldn't say that. It might

have set the tone for how we interacted with each other. But I never knew when to hold my tongue then, and you had every right to tell me to mind my own business."

"Maybe so. I think I pushed you away, and I never intended to do that." Opening up to Brooke like this wasn't easy. Chess was tempted to stop there, but he forged ahead. It had to have been hard for her when she revealed her original hopes for her future, or called him from the bar last night when she could've summoned a cab. She'd made an effort this week, and he wanted to do the same.

"You wanted to know what landed me in foster care." He had her full attention and continued. "When I was a kid, I lived in Dallas and my home life was a mess. My parents fought all the time. I'm talking shouting fights and verbal abuse on an almost daily basis. My father was a drunk and spent most of his time lying around the house, semi-conscious. My mother loathed it, though she wasn't much better. She was rarely happy. I remember her crying more than anything else."

Brooke frowned. "I'm sorry."

He shrugged. "My little brother, Nathan, was born when I was five. If anything, our mother seemed even sadder after that. As an adult looking back, I'm sure she was depressed. Some days, she didn't even want to get out of bed. We had little food or money. Most of the time, I ended up taking care of Nathan. I fed him, changed his diapers, and everything else."

Brooke listened intently, her chin cupped in one of her hands. Her eyes were wide as though she were nervous about what he would say next.

"When the fights escalated, I'd take Nathan

into our room and close the door. Sometimes, we didn't go back out for hours. One day, before Nathan was a year old, I woke up and our mother was gone. We never saw her again. I asked my father several times where she was and he always said things were too much for her and that she had to start over."

"Oh, Chess. That's horrible!"

Sometimes not knowing what happened was worse than the facts themselves. Except Chess still didn't know what happened to his mother and only had speculation. He'd kept all these memories buried deep. Now that they were surfacing, some of the other details he'd forgotten were coming to mind as well. Like the musty smell of his bedroom, or the liquor-infused breath of his father. "I'd done everything I could to take care of Nathan. I promised him I would. I blamed myself for not having done enough sometimes, especially when he'd cry because he was hungry and I had nothing to give him." He held up a hand to stop her when she started to speak. "Thinking about it now, I realize I did way more than any six-year-old should've had to do. But at the time..."

"It makes sense you'd feel that way. I never knew my dad, and I have few memories of him. But I still grew up wondering if I'd done something to make him leave."

He nodded. "Exactly. My father only drank more after that. When I was eight and Nathan was three, we had no money, and my father got desperate. He robbed a liquor store and stabbed the owner with a knife. He went to jail, and social services came and got me and Nathan."

Brooke cringed. What was she thinking? Did she pity him? He sure hoped not — that was the last thing he wanted.

"I promised myself that day I would be there for Nathan. That I would never leave him like our mother did, and that I would put him first like our father should have." He'd sure fallen short of fulfilling those pledges to his brother. He suppressed the tidal wave of failure that threatened to crash over him.

Brooke listened to Chess's story, her heart breaking for the little boy he once was. Losing one parent, no matter what the cause, was hard enough. But two was even more devastating. She imagined Chess watching over his baby brother when he was little more than a baby himself.

He'd never mentioned Nathan before. What happened to him? She wanted to ask but kept quiet. It was big that Chess was even telling her about all of this, and she didn't want to push him. He'd tell her when or if he was ready.

"I remember the day a social worker came and got me," she said. "It was overwhelming and confusing." She paused. "I guess we both entered the system at eight, didn't we?"

Chess nodded. "I hadn't realized that. But yeah, I guess we did." He observed her as though he were deciding how much more to reveal.

"It's okay. You don't have to tell me anything else if you don't want to."

"I appreciate that, Brooke. But it's probably something I should have shared a long time ago." He stared at the coffee table. "We bounced from foster home to foster home for six months until we ended up with a family that had five other kids besides us, all of them older than I was. I took care of Nathan the best that I could, and I hated having to go to school during the day and leaving him with our foster parents. One morning, a social worker came to the house. Apparently, our foster parents had expressed concern about Nathan staying there with all the older kids. I was told there were no homes that would take both of us and that Nathan needed to live somewhere else." His voice broke. "I tried to stop them. My foster father had to hold me back to keep me from running after Nathan. I remember the social worker had to carry him away because he was crying my name." He raked a hand through his hair and let out a slow breath. "I was told they would help us stay in touch, but that never happened. I didn't know where Nathan went. Maybe it was a miscommunication. But I spent the rest of my childhood wondering whether Nathan was okay. When I turned fifteen, I ran away and searched for him. It was like he'd just disappeared."

Brooke held a hand to her mouth, her eyes stung with unshed tears. It'd been bad enough going through what she did, much less being separated from a sibling. Especially one she'd been caring for like Chess had Nathan. "That's horrible. I can't even imagine … What were the caseworkers thinking, splitting you guys up like that? And not even letting you stay in touch? That's messed up."

Chess nodded, his teeth clenched. "I was upset about it for years. The anger and effort to find him consumed me."

"Why are you telling me all of this now?" She said it gently and hoped it didn't come off like she was accusing him or upset at him for not telling her sooner.

He paused. "Because my brother contacted me online this week."

Brooke gasped. "You're kidding!"

"It seems he got adopted, and his last name was changed. His family later moved to Florida, which is why I haven't been able to find him. I wouldn't have known where to look." There was no missing the pain in his eyes.

"Did you explain to him what happened?" Brooke already knew the answer, otherwise Chess would be happier about finding his brother.

"He says they told him I didn't want to go with him, and that's why he was alone. I said that wasn't true, but I don't think he's ready to hear what actually happened. I'm trying to give him time. I don't want him to break contact, not after thinking I'd never speak to him again."

Brooke thought for a moment. "We don't understand what happened to him once he was removed from that home. If he grew up thinking you didn't want him, it would be hard to let that go." Chess was frowning, and she reached across the couch to touch his hand, trying to ignore the warmth that spread through her chest in response. "Give him time. If he bothered to locate and contact you, he'll eventually want to know your side of things. He's probably having to work up the courage."

"I hope you're right. After everything we went through, the last thing I wanted to lose was my only family. He was four and probably barely remembers me." Chess looked at their joined hands as though he only just realized she was touching him. He turned his over and held hers a moment before giving it a gentle squeeze and letting go.

Brooke's heart jumped into her throat. "I'm glad you told me about Nathan, Chess. I'll be praying everything will work itself out."

He frowned at her. "Brooke…"

"I know you don't believe and that's okay. I'll still be praying."

He gave a single nod and stood. "Thanks for listening. I'm sorry I didn't tell you back when you first asked me."

"It's okay. I get it." She wished he had, too. What would their friendship be like now if that had been the case? It meant a lot he'd finally told her about it now. "And I'm glad we had dinner. I missed that last weekend. It's weird to think Anna and Joel will be home in a little over a week." She would miss the one-on-one time with Chess.

"Yeah, it is." He paused, and they stood there for several moments in heavy silence. "It's been nice spending time just the two of us."

Brooke agreed. "We don't do that very often, do we?" She ran her fingertip along the edge of a nearby bookshelf. A thin layer of dust she could barely see collected on her skin. "Maybe we could make a point of hanging out once in a while even after Joel and Anna get back. It might be fun."

"Might, huh? I'd have thought you'd be getting tired of me by now." Chess winked at her.

Not hardly. If anything, it'd made her look forward to seeing him even more next time. She wrinkled her nose. "Nah, not yet. Give it time, though."

Chess chuckled. He reached out to her dust-covered finger and used his own hand to brush it clean. "I guess I'm slacking in the housekeeping department now that I'm the only one here. At least Epic hasn't complained."

She drew in a sharp breath at the connection and quickly clasped her hands together.

Chess cleared his throat. "Speaking of Epic, I'm going to take him to the park tomorrow. I meant to do it all week and didn't have the time. I don't suppose you'd like to go with us."

Brooke couldn't have been more surprised by the invitation. "I get off work at three. I could meet you there."

They finished settling their plans and then said their goodbyes before Brooke headed home. Her chest expanded and she let out a whoosh of air. She could still feel the way his hand had briefly held hers. And he'd finally shared about his past. Had he told Joel yet? She didn't think so, and that made her feel special. Like she was more than the annoying little sister he was always having to get out of scrapes.

She'd spent a long time trying to distance herself from her mixed-up emotions concerning Chess. But tonight, she had renewed hope. It probably wasn't a good thing, but she couldn't keep the smile off her face all the same.

Chapter Six

Chess was on his way to the park where he'd arranged to meet Brooke. It was a little warm, but the sky was full of clouds which helped block some of the sun's rays. It was only the first week of September, and they still had a while to go before fall weather hit this area of Texas.

He thought about their conversation the evening before. He'd been nervous to tell her about Nathan and what happened to him as a child. But she'd listened without judging. He should have told her and Joel ages ago. A weight he hadn't realized he'd been carrying eased a little.

After the last couple of days, Chess felt closer to Brooke than he'd ever been before. Briefly holding her hand last night had felt nicer than it probably should have. She was beginning to confide in him a little. He'd wanted a better relationship between them, and now it appeared that might become a reality.

He wouldn't trick himself into thinking there could be any more than that. She saw him as a big brother. He'd already failed in that role once with Nathan, he wasn't about to let Brooke down now. So, he'd bury his feelings for her like he always had and be thankful for the closer relationship they were developing.

He located her Kia and pulled into a spot next to it. He'd barely stepped out of his truck when Epic bounded after him. No one else was around. Chess threw a tennis ball and watched as the dog tore after it. "He loves going to the park." He bent to accept the ball when Epic brought it back. "Anna tells me this is one of his favorite things."

Epic bounced on his hind legs and landed on all four again, eyes bright and mouth open. The ball barely left Chess's hand before Epic was racing across the grass after it.

Chess walked beside Brooke as she followed the dog. "It's nice there isn't anyone else around here so we can let him run."

"It is a peaceful park." She picked up the ball that Epic dropped at her feet and lobbed it into the air again. She turned her head and looked at him. "Are you doing okay today?"

He knew she was talking about last night. He nodded. "Thanks for listening. I appreciate it."

"Of course." She focused on the Great Pyrenees. "Have you heard from Nathan?"

He blew out a lungful of air. "Not a word today. He said he would be busy this week though. If I don't hear from him before long, I may try to track down his phone number. I'll probably wait and see what Joel thinks."

"So, you'll tell him about everything?"

"Yeah. I should've told you both a long time

ago. Sometimes it's strange how years can drag, yet disappear in a blink of an eye." They say time heals all wounds. Chess wasn't sure of that. He noted the bruise on Brooke's face and was happy to see it was fading already. "Has anyone commented about your bruise at work?"

Brooke's hand touched her cheek. "I cover it up with make-up. No one's even noticed." She stopped and clapped her hands together. "Epic, come back here."

The dog had caught a whiff of something and his curiosity led him farther than he should probably go. It took another clap before he lifted his head and took off at a run toward them. Instead of slowing down, he barreled right into Brooke's legs and knocked her off balance.

Chess reached out and grasped her around the waist before she fell, holding her against himself as she regained her footing. She turned in his arms and lifted her chin.

"Thanks." Her voice sounded breathless.

The breeze blew some of her hair into her face. Without thinking, Chess brushed it back with his hand and tucked it behind her ear. A hint of her rose-scented shampoo combined with sunshine and freshly mowed grass. His heart thudded painfully against his ribs in response to her still standing there in his arms. "You okay?"

She nodded and took a step back, her cheeks coloring. She frowned at Epic who was completely oblivious to nearly bowling her over. "They need to put a warning sign on him."

Chess chuckled. "That's not a bad idea." He threw the ball for Epic who didn't hesitate to chase it down.

Brooke's phone pinged. She withdrew it, checked the screen, and scowled. She jabbed out a text message and sent it before stuffing it into her pocket again. "Larry. I said I was done and didn't want to see him again. He's been apologizing since Thursday."

Chess frowned. He didn't care if the guy had apologized a thousand times. If she told him their relationship was over, he needed to leave her alone. "Block his number, Brooke. He needs to take no for an answer. If he can't, there's no reason you should continue to have to deal with him." She seemed to hesitate, and that frustrated him. "Why do you let these guys run over you like this?" The words were out before he could stop them. But it was something he'd thought about a lot over the last few months when he'd hear about the less-than-stellar guys she dated. The dark expression she shot his way only confirmed he should've kept his mouth shut.

Her eyebrows flew upwards, and she folded her arms in front of her chest. "That's not fair. I don't let them run me over. If I did that, I'd have stayed in that bar the other night. Or had some drinks. If I was that much of a pushover, I'd have slept with some of the jerks I've met in the last year." Her voice rose in pitch as she talked. "So, don't start with me. My relationships are none of your business."

Chess was aware this was when Joel would step in and put a stop to the conversation before it got messy. He longed for their friend to be there now. "I care about you, Brooke. That makes it my business. I want you to be happy."

Her shoulders fell. "Don't you think I want that, too?"

Epic dropped the ball at Chess's feet, ignored. Chess focused all his attention on Brooke. "Then why do you keep dating these messed up guys? There's got to be some decent men in this town. What's wrong with them?"

Brooke sucked her bottom lip in and worried it between her teeth. It seemed like she was gazing everywhere but at him.

Chess bent down to glimpse her face, refusing to move until she lifted her gaze to his. "Talk to me. Why do you keep doing this to yourself?"

"It doesn't matter who I date." Her words were barely above a whisper.

"Why?"

Tears pooled in her dark brown eyes as they begged him to understand. "Because they aren't you."

Chess stared at Brooke. What was she talking about, saying the other guys weren't him? She couldn't possibly mean... Her words crashed through his fog of confusion. No. He had to be misunderstanding her. But even as he tried to reconcile in his mind what he heard with his ears, he could see the truth on her face.

There were many times he'd buried how he felt about Brooke, tamped it down and kept it hidden. He'd failed Nathan, but he was determined to be there for Brooke. Be the friend she needed and the big brother he'd been certain she saw him as. He'd never entertained the idea she might feel something more for him. How had he missed this?

Uncertainty danced with sadness in Brooke's eyes. But it was the hope there that effectively stabbed Chess right in the heart and twisted the dagger for emphasis.

They'd scarcely begun to develop the closeness

he'd missed. She was talking to him, confiding in him. The horrible things his parents yelled at each other filled his head. He'd decided long ago that having a wife and family wasn't for him. The thought of it even resembling what he grew up with scared him.

She'd told him about her dream of getting married and being a stay at home mom. He clenched his jaw and steeled himself for what he was about to say.

"Brooke, you deserve that family you've always wanted. The doting husband and a house full of kids. You deserve it all." *You deserve someone better than me.* He allowed himself to run the back of his hand along her cheek before letting it drop to his side. "I wish… It's something I can't give you. I'm sorry."

Pain flashed across her face. She pressed a hand to her stomach, her eyebrows drawn together as she let her gaze fall. "I know if I'd only…"

"No." Chess's word came out harsher than he'd intended, but it brought her eyes back to his. "It's not you."

At those words, she huffed and shook her head.

"I know. I know that's what people say all the time. But it's the truth here. I wouldn't be good for you, Brooke. You deserve more."

"That's not true. Chess, if you'll give us a chance…"

"I can't." He watched as her face paled. The emotional walls came up, and Brooke shut herself off from him. He felt the loss as keenly as if she'd disappeared into thin air. "You're one of the most important people in my life. You understand that, don't you?" When she said nothing, he put a hand on her shoulder. "Brooke?"

"Sure." But there was sarcasm in her voice. She moved as if in slow motion. "I'm going to head home."

Chess's chest tightened, and a headache pounded behind his eyes. "I'm sorry, Brooke." He wanted to say more but didn't have the words. Against all instincts, he watched her get into her car and pull out of the parking lot.

He told himself she'd eventually come to see he was right. She deserved more than he could give her.

And she was everything he'd ever wanted.

When Brooke woke up, she couldn't quite figure out why all the lights were on in the apartment. Or why she was still dressed and curled up on the couch. What day was it? And then everything that happened at the park with Chess came rushing back to her.

Her head ached and her stomach rolled. How could she have been so monumentally idiotic? Why did she have to open her mouth? She should've insisted it was because she was bad with men. Or because she was cursed. Anything would've been better than referring to how she felt about him. She ran a hand through the mess of tangles in her hair and then covered her eyes. Oh, she'd probably give almost anything right now if it meant she could go back and change what she'd said.

His voice echoed in her head.

"It's something I can't give you."

Of course he couldn't. Because he didn't care about her like that. She'd known that fact for a long time. Yet, until he'd said it, she'd been able to pretend there was hope. Brooke hadn't realized that until now, and it made her feel even worse. She'd been holding onto a dumb dream like a lovesick kid.

Well, if Chess didn't think of her as an immature child before, he sure had to now. She might've cried again except there couldn't possibly be any tears left. Her eyelids felt puffy and thick. Boy, she wasn't about to examine herself in the mirror right now.

What time was it? Brooke reached for her phone on the coffee table. Two in the morning. And there were three more texts from Larry. Chess was right about one thing — she needed to block Larry's number and end this. She'd already said she was done and didn't want to see him anymore. So, she went into her recent calls and made sure she'd receive no more communication from him.

Chess was also right about how she dated too much. Every time she went out with a guy, it was a desperate hope that she'd finally find someone who would take the place of Chess. But now she knew that she'd been searching for something that didn't exist. Maybe she should convert to Catholicism and become a nun, swear off men completely.

With that thought, she allowed herself to fall backwards onto the couch again. What was she going to say to him? Would he even be able to look at her without seeing her as completely pathetic?

Yep, moving to a convent was sounding better and better. She needed to do something different. Her goals in life had grown stagnant. When did that happen? Chess was right. Maybe she needed to consider a change in career.

She got up from the couch and wandered into

the bathroom to wash her face and caught her reflection in the mirror. Her career wasn't the only thing that could use a transformation.

At least it was Sunday, and she didn't have to worry about seeing him until next weekend if she didn't want to.

Not wanting to think about anything, she curled up on her bed and tried her best to fall asleep again.

Chapter Seven

Brooke forced the frown from her face when she walked into the salon Tuesday morning. Jasmine glanced up and waved. "I still love what we did with your hair. I hope you got some retail therapy in last night. There's nothing like a new pair of shoes or dress to go with a fresh hairdo."

After everything with Chess, work was a welcome distraction for Brooke. She'd even forgotten about Larry until he walked through the front door later that day. She was in the middle of cutting her customer's hair when he approached her, cupped her elbow, and leaned in close. "I'd like to speak to you for a few minutes, please."

She shifted her elbow away from him, not appreciating the familiar gesture. "I'm right in the middle of this. You'll have to wait."

He didn't say a word, simply strode over to a chair on the other side of the room and sat, giving her a pointed stare.

Brooke suppressed a sigh, smiled at Mrs. Jones

in the mirror, and kept on cutting. She was keenly aware of the attention the exchange with Larry had attracted. When Mrs. Jones was happy with her hair, she paid Brooke and included a nice tip.

Unfortunately, Larry was still waiting and Brooke had over a half hour until her next customer would be in. This time, she didn't even hold back the sigh. "Jasmine, I'm taking ten. I'll be back soon."

Jasmine raised a hand in acknowledgment.

Brooke grabbed her bag. Larry stood as she approached and motioned to the door. They walked outside. "We can sit in my car and talk."

Yeah, that's not happening. "I think right here is good." Brooke crossed her arms in front of her and leaned against the outer wall of the building. "What do you want, Larry?"

"You wouldn't call me back."

Way to state the obvious. "I told you to quit calling me. It didn't work between us."

To his credit, Larry seemed embarrassed. "I've never done something like that before. I don't understand what happened."

"You got drunk at a bar, ignored your date, and then hit her with a pool cue." She raised an eyebrow at him. Apparently, some of her people skills had been decimated right along with her confidence over the last two weeks.

The expression on his face shifted to shame and then desperation. "It truly was an accident. I didn't realize it hit you that hard, or I would've taken you home or gotten you some ice. Something. I apologize for that." His eyes begged her to believe him.

Maybe what he said was true. But he still went to the bar after they'd made plans. And he still got drunk and didn't bother to make sure Brooke got home okay. As far as she was concerned, he could be sorry to the moon and back. They were done. "I appreciate the apology. But like I said, I don't think this can work. We're too different." Brooke gave a little shrug. "I wish you all the best, Larry. I've got to get back to work."

He protested, but she turned and walked back inside. When he didn't follow, she released a sigh of relief. Hopefully that would be the end of it. Chess would be proud of the way she put her foot down.

Chess. She hadn't talked to him since the park. He was in Dallas at his office right now. Normally, she'd text him merely to say hi. Less than two weeks ago, she wouldn't have hesitated and Brooke hated that she did now. She missed him more than she'd ever thought possible.

It was Friday evening and Chess hadn't stopped thinking about Brooke all week. He'd stayed busy at work — probably too much so. Their deadline came and went without much of a hitch. But not seeing or talking to Brooke was driving him crazy. He disliked not knowing how she was doing.

He wished he hadn't pushed her about Larry. Maybe if he'd been more understanding and less accusatory when it came to her dating choices, the whole topic wouldn't have come up in the first place.

How was he supposed to act the next time he saw her? This time last week, he had no idea she thought of him as any more than her annoying, over-protective friend. But now… It would be much easier if she'd never told him. Where did that leave them?

He blinked at the episode he was watching on TV. After binge watching for several hours, he doubted he could recall more than five minutes of what had happened. Instead, their conversation at the park kept replaying itself in his head.

Joel and Anna should arrive home late tonight. With the time change and all, he suspected it would take a while for them to get caught up. But they were supposed to all meet at Chess's house Sunday afternoon. Joel insisted he and Anna would bring something to eat. Would Brooke act like nothing happened when they were all together? Would she even talk to him?

What if she'd rather avoid the event entirely?

That last thought bothered him more than anything else. Guilt and confusion fought for top billing on his emotions.

He picked up his cell phone and began to text Brooke like he had numerous times through the week. He'd always deleted his messages before.

"Are you okay? I've missed you this week. Will you be coming over on Sunday as planned?"

This time, he hit send before he talked himself out of it and then held his breath for a response.

Ten minutes later, she sent one back. *"I'll be there."*

And that was it. No sign of where they stood. Yeah, seeing each other for the first time since the park, and in the company of their friends, probably wasn't the best idea.

Saturday wasn't much better. Epic must have sensed his unease because the poor dog kept following Chess around with a look of worry on his face. By

Sunday afternoon, Chess was ready to get everybody there. Surely this would be one of those situations where worrying about it was much worse than what he was actually dreading.

There was a knock at the door and when he opened it, he found Brooke standing on the other side. She clutched a cake pan like a shield in front of her. Chess took note of her hair and paused. She'd cut at least two inches off and then had thick, blonde highlights added. He couldn't remember the last time she dyed her hair but it'd been a while. The timing was anything but a coincidence.

Brooke balanced the pan with one hand and put the other on her head as if she were self-conscious about her hair. Did she regret the change? He looked closely and could no longer see the bruise on her face. At least that wound had healed, unlike the rift between them which had only gotten bigger in the last week.

The vulnerability in her eyes warred with stubborn pride when her gaze met his. "Hey. I guess I got here first."

Chess nodded. "They're running a few minutes late." He reached for the pan. "Let me get that for you." She hesitated before relinquishing it to him.

Epic trotted up to the door, and Brooke immediately bent down to pet him. "I'll bet you'll be glad to see Anna, won't you? She should be here any minute." She entered the house then, moving to the couch so she could continue to give Epic attention.

Chess took the pan into the kitchen and lifted the plastic lid. The apple crisp must have come out of the oven not long before she came over because the glass container it was in was still warm. The scent of cinnamon and apples made his stomach growl. With a deep breath to steady his nerves, he wandered back to the living room.

"The dessert smells amazing. I think I have some vanilla ice cream in the freezer we can have with it."

She nodded, her attention still on the dog. "That sounds good." Her voice was quiet.

Chess didn't like how awkward it was to be around Brooke right now.

"Brooke, I wish I knew what to say…"

Epic barked, his ears turning toward the door. A moment later, he was running in that direction.

"That must be them." Brooke jumped to her feet and followed the dog. Chess trailed behind them.

Brooke opened the door to reveal their friends wearing colorful Hawaiian shirts and bright smiles. The moment Anna saw Epic, she crouched to give the dog a hug. Epic wasted no time in knocking her down and lavishing her face with kisses.

Laughter filled the air as Joel took her hand, hauling her back to her feet. There were hugs all around and they all filed back into Chess's living room.

Brooke embraced them both for a second time. "I'm happy for you guys. Did you have an amazing trip? You'll have to tell us all about it." She took a step back and her gaze fell on their joined hands. "Check you two out."

Anna blushed. Joel chuckled, put an arm around Anna's shoulder, and then placed a kiss to her cheek. "We missed you guys. We brought gifts." He held up two bags and waved them back and forth.

Chess took in Brooke's genuine smile as she accepted the bag Joel handed to her. He'd missed that carefree grin this last week. Something touched his arm, and he realized Joel was trying to hand a bag to him with a raised eyebrow.

Ignoring the unspoken question, Chess took it and pulled out a t-shirt that read, *"My friends went to Hawaii and all I got was this shirt."* He laughed. "Thank you for this." He shook his head and pulled out the other item in the bottom of the bag. He lifted the top off the rectangular box and marveled at the knife and its intricately-carved wooden handle. "Wow, this is beautiful. Thank you both."

Joel reached over and pulled a business card out of the box. "This guy makes all of them by hand. We saw him at a show we went to and knew we had to bring one back."

Chess hefted the knife in one hand and admired the way the light reflected off the shiny blade. "He does incredible work. I appreciate this."

Anna was pulling Brooke's hair back and fastening it with an intricate metal clip. "There we go. And your hair is pretty like this. When did you have it done?"

"Monday. I had Jasmine at work cut and color it for me." Brooke reached a hand back to feel the clip and then gave Chess a shy glance before turning her attention back to her friend. She lifted a colorful snow globe depicting an underwater scene. "You two are sweet. You shouldn't have brought us gifts. But thank you, these are lovely."

"You're welcome." The newly-married couple exchanged a glimpse of adoration.

Chess wondered what it would be like to love someone so much that you could make that kind of commitment. That wasn't in the cards for him, but it didn't mean he couldn't wish it were different. He focused on Brooke and caught her wiping at one of her eyes. She noticed his attention and turned away as she and Anna talked about Hawaii.

Joel had also been watching Brooke and frowned. He tipped his head toward the door. "We brought pizza. Want to help me bring it in?"

"Sure." Chess took in a deep breath of fresh air as they returned outside. He hadn't realized how stuffy it'd gotten in the house.

Joel led the way to his car, but before he opened the door, he turned. "Is everything okay with Brooke? Something seems a little off with her."

Chess hadn't expected that. Everything between him and Brooke would have to come out in the open eventually, but he'd hoped to avoid it for at least today.

"I take it her date with that guy didn't work out well."

There was the out Chess needed. He resisted the urge to release a sigh of relief. "The guy turned out to be a real piece of work." Briefly, he told Joel about that evening and how Larry had treated Brooke.

Joel didn't seem to be any happier about it than Chess had been. "If he knows what's good for him, he'll keep his distance."

Chess gave a nod and bit his tongue. He sincerely hoped Brooke blocked the guy's number or put him in his place, but he didn't know and he wasn't about to say anything else. He helped Joel with the boxes of pizza.

Once back inside, everyone settled down to eat. With Anna and Joel telling them about their trip, Brooke and Chess didn't have to say much as they all chatted through dinner. Chess didn't miss the fact that

Brooke seemed to look everywhere but at him. He bit back a sigh of frustration.

When they had their fill of pizza, conversation lulled. Joel studied first Chess and then Brooke. "Did something happen while we were gone?" When no one responded, his curious expression turned to one of concern. "What's going on?"

Brooke's cheeks turned pink. Chess's own ears grew hot. He'd hoped he could avoid this conversation. In fact, he'd hoped that they'd all get together this afternoon and everything between him and Brooke would be a non-issue. Though the moment he saw her, he knew that would never happen.

Brooke's eyes widened, and she threw a frantic look in Chess's direction. Tears filled her eyes. She jumped to her feet and muttered a quick, "Please excuse me for a minute," on the way out of the room. Epic jumped to his feet and ran toward the sound of the back door opening.

Chess focused on the chair Brooke vacated and nausea rolled through his stomach.

And there were Joel and Anna, staring at him. Waiting for an explanation. What was he supposed to say? He held up both hands. "It's my fault. But she could probably use someone to go out there with her, and it can't be me."

Anna exchanged a glance with Joel and nodded. "I'll check on her."

When she left, Joel's expression combined concern with accusation. "What on earth happened between you two?"

With little choice, Chess filled him in on everything that had happened between him and Brooke over the last week or so.

Joel shook his head. "Well, I suppose that was bound to happen, eventually."

Chess couldn't have been more surprised by what his friend said. "You mean, you knew she felt that way about me?"

"It was obvious. It has been for a long time." Joel's mouth transformed into a wide grin.

"Then why didn't I know? Why didn't you say something? The two of you are so close, until Anna came along, I figured you'd end up together."

Joel laughed loudly at that. "I have always considered her my sister. And you're lying to yourself if you ever thought otherwise." He shrugged. "I think Brooke has tried real hard to ignore how she felt. I figured you were, too. Or something, I don't know. But you two work the way you are. Were." He sobered. "You know Brooke. Things will never be the same now."

"I know." Chess didn't need Joel to tell him that. He ran a hand over his face.

"Are you saying you don't care about her that way?"

Chess cast a furtive glance toward the backyard and lowered his voice. "It doesn't matter. It never has. I told her about my past and how I ended up in foster care. I need to tell you, too. But suffice it to say, getting married and having a happily ever after isn't in my future. I didn't mean to hurt Brooke, but I did. And she can hold a wicked grudge." He slouched in his chair and leaned his head back. "She probably hates me."

"I don't blame you. I have things about my childhood I've still told no one except for maybe Anna. And I guarantee Brooke does, too." Joel jabbed a thumb in their friend's direction. "She doesn't hate you anymore than I do. But you'll have to give her time to digest everything. She probably feels like she's lost you."

Chess's mind raced, and he knew exactly what Joel meant. That's how he felt about Brooke right now. If Brooke truly didn't hate him — and he still wasn't convinced of that — he hoped she'd understand someday. Their new-found closer friendship was probably gone for good. It was strange how much he was mourning what he'd only had for a couple of weeks.

Joel cleared his throat. "You are both incredibly stubborn, to say the least." He pressed his lips together. "I'm staying out of whatever this is between you. But I do want to say this: Think long and hard about burning any bridges with Brooke. They'll be real hard to build back up again."

Chess knew that was true. "I'll work on cleaning all this up if you want to go out and talk to her."

Joel nodded. "I'll be back in a few minutes."

Chess gathered the dishes and carried them into the kitchen. He tried to push images of Brooke crying out of his head because he didn't think his heart could take it.

Chapter Eight

The sliding glass patio door opened, and Joel stepped into the backyard. "Mind if I join you?"

Brooke shook her head and tried to compose herself. She'd already spilled what happened to Anna while crying. She couldn't do it again. Anna rubbed her back while Joel sat down in a chair next to them.

Anna and Joel exchanged a look, and Brooke fanned her face to try to cool herself down. Her poor friends had come home from an amazing honeymoon and were left trying to clean up an emotional mess from both her and Chess. Not much of a welcome.

Joel reached out and gently squeezed her arm.

Brooke sighed. "I'm assuming Chess probably told you everything?" He nodded. *Good.* She glanced at Anna. "I was telling Anna I may join a convent. Somewhere off in the forest or something."

Joel gave a quiet chuckle. "You and I both know you'd never make it out in the forest. You should land a city convent."

He was right, and if it reduced the chances of

ever running into Chess again, she didn't care where it was. Even though she fought against it, a smile won over. Brooke groaned. "How do I always end up in these messes?"

"You don't. It only feels that way sometimes." Joel gave her a hug before he put an arm around Anna.

Brooke observed the couple. "You two realize that you're so cute together, it's almost sickening, right?" The three of them laughed, and she had to admit it felt good. "Is Chess okay?"

Joel hesitated. "He's worried about you. It's Chess: he's tough and doesn't like to let his emotions show through. He's pretty upset about the whole thing."

She doubted it. Chess always seemed to know what to do. Thinking about it now, Brooke realized she leaned on that all the time. Probably not a good thing. It was time she stopped relying on everyone else and dealt with her own problems for a change.

"What's up with the hair?" Joel indicated Brooke's head.

Brooke put both hands on her hair and groaned. "Spontaneous and stupid. Be honest and tell me how bad it really is."

Anna spoke up quickly. "I told you, it's pretty. Very different, and sometimes that's exactly what we need. I like it."

Joel nodded. "It looks good on you. I don't remember the last time you did something with your hair."

Yet another sign of how stuck in a rut she'd become. Her thoughts must have been on her face because Joel reached out and squeezed her arm. "Things will be okay. Maybe not the same, but okay."

Right. Try to go back to the way she acted around Chess all the time before last weekend. She could do that. She had to — for him and for her own sanity as well. How come that fact didn't take away the longing and sting of rejection? *God, please show me how to move past this.*

Anna stood and gave her a hug. "Why don't you come in and have some of that dessert you brought? It smells amazing."

"I think I just want to head home. I hope you guys don't mind."

They all stood, and Joel led the way to the door. "Of course not."

Brooke nodded and went inside. She got her bag then gave her newlywed friends another hug. "It's good to have you guys home. You were missed, but I'm glad you had such a great time. Thanks again for the gifts."

Chess came out of the kitchen then, his brows creased. "Are you leaving?"

So much for hoping she could sneak out without having to talk to Chess again. "Yeah, I think I should." She gave what she hoped was a relaxed wave. "I'll talk to you all later."

She hadn't even made it as far as the driveway before Chess jogged out after her. "Brooke, please wait."

Brooke held up a hand. "I don't want to talk. I need to go home and put this humiliating day behind me. Okay?"

Hurt shadowed his eyes. "I hate you don't feel like you can stay."

She shrugged. "It is what it is, right?" Certain her own wounded expression matched his pound for pound, she got in her car and drove away. With eyes burning from all the tears and a heart heavy with confusion and grief, she focused on getting home.

Four blocks from her apartment, the blaring sound of a horn barely registered before she whipped her head to the right. A black car raced through the red light toward the middle of the intersection where Brooke was driving through. She braced herself for the impact there was no way she could avoid.

A sickening crunch filled her ears as pain shot through her body and into her shoulder. Brooke let her head fall back against the seat. Acrid smoke filled the air, a car horn wouldn't quit, and every time she tried to focus on something, only a blurry image filled her vision.

Someone jerked her car door open. "Miss? Are you okay?"

Brooke tried to turn and see who was speaking to her. But merely thinking about moving made her head pound. "I don't think so..." She inhaled, resulting in a sharp pain piercing her side. Blackness crowded in as the surrounding noises faded away.

Chess watched as Brooke's tail lights disappeared. He couldn't get the image of Brooke's face, eyes downcast and red from crying, out of his head. It killed him that he was responsible for that. All he'd ever wanted was to see Brooke happy and yet, here they were.

Hopefully having Joel and Anna to talk to had helped her tonight. She hadn't wanted to stay because of him and it left him with a hole in his chest. If she

was anywhere near as miserable as he was right now…
For the hundredth time, he wished things had gone
differently.

He went back inside and dished out dessert for
his friends. Thankfully, they didn't bring up the
situation between him and Brooke. It mattered little
though. Knowing they were eating the dessert she
made while she wasn't there enjoying it, too, weighed
on all of them.

Twenty minutes later, Chess waved goodbye to
the newlyweds as they left for home.

At his computer, a message from Nathan
caught his attention immediately.

"I'd like to come visit for a while."

Chess blinked at the words. He wanted to visit?
For how long? Chess hadn't even mentioned where he
lived, only that it was in Texas. A far cry from Florida.
Although Nathan could probably locate Chess's
address if he tried.

"How long would you be able to stay?"

Chess didn't want to offend him, but needed to
know before he said yes to anything.

"I'm hoping for a week."

Meeting Nathan conjured a combination of
nerves and eagerness. *I think that'd be great. If you'll let me
know when you might arrive, I can be sure to pick you up from
the airport.*

*"I may like the area enough to move there. I think it
might be time for a change. Maybe find a new job. I've heard
everything's bigger there in Texas."* That was followed by a
winking emoji.

"What's going on?" Chess would prefer more
details before inviting the guy to come up here with the
rest of his family.

"I'd rather talk to you in person. If I got a flight in this coming weekend, would that be too early?"

Chess's eyebrows lifted. He hadn't expected it to be this soon. *"I'm pretty sure I should have no problem scheduling time off. Let me check with work tomorrow, and I'll let you know for sure."*

"Sounds good."

They chatted for another minute or two before ending the conversation. Chess would see his long-lost brother again.

He was heading into the living room when his phone rang. "Hey, Joel. Long time no talk. What's up?"

"Chess? Brooke was in a car accident. We're on our way to the hospital now."

"What?" Chess was out the door and in his truck in moments. "Is she okay? What happened?"

"Someone ran a red light and hit her passenger side." He spoke to someone in the background. "Anastasia says they wouldn't release any more information over the phone except to say she was at the hospital."

Chess cursed. "I'll meet you guys there."

"Be safe. You can't help her if you kill yourself getting there. We're pulling in, I'm going to go."

"Yeah."

The line went quiet, and Chess tossed his phone into the passenger seat.

He reached the hospital in what he was sure had to be record time. He located Joel and Anna in the second floor waiting area. "How is she?"

Joel cringed. "We don't know. They assured us a doctor would be out to update us as soon as possible."

"What's that supposed to mean?" Chess

resisted the urge to go to the nurse's station and demand more information. Surely Brooke's condition wasn't as bad as what his imagination was summoning up right now. "Did you guys get to see her?"

Anna shook her head. "They wouldn't let us. They said she's unconscious." Her eyes filled with tears.

"What about the other driver?"

Joel put an arm around Anna and pulled her close. "He's in worse shape. I guess he got a text and glanced down at it. Completely missed the light turning red."

Chess's stomach rolled.

Joel took his arm and directed him to a set of chairs. They all sat down.

Chess was vaguely aware of Joel and Anna praying together for Brooke. Meanwhile, he couldn't focus on anything, his mind and body numb. If Brooke had sustained internal damage... He couldn't let his thoughts go that direction. The idea of losing her stole the oxygen from his lungs.

They waited nearly an hour before a doctor came into the waiting room. "Are you the family of Brooke Pierce?"

All three of them stood. Chess took several steps forward. "Yes. Is she okay?"

"The impact threw Miss Pierce against the door. She has a laceration on her head that required five stitches to close." The doctor held up a hand to reassure them, anticipating some of their questions. "We took her in for a CT scan. She has a concussion, but there is no damage otherwise." The doctor glanced at his iPad and scanned what was on the screen. "She has three broken ribs on her left side. There is no immediate danger of the ribs damaging any of her organs, but she'll be sore for a while. We'd like to keep her here for observation tonight. She should be able to go home tomorrow."

"Thank goodness," Anna breathed.

"Can we see her?" The question came from Joel.

"I believe they are taking her into recovery. Someone should be here soon to take you back so you can sit with her. I've given her something for the pain, therefore she'll probably sleep for a while. I'll be by later, too, and I can answer any of Miss Pierce's questions." The surgeon shook hands with both Chess and Joel.

Chess sat down again and massaged the back of his neck. "This is all my fault."

Joel took the seat beside him. "Don't even go there. This had nothing to do with you."

Chess clenched his jaw and turned abruptly toward Joel. "If I'd handled everything better, Brooke would've stayed for dessert, and she wouldn't have been in the accident in the first place." He was supposed to protect Brooke, be there for her, and keep her safe. Instead, she landed in the hospital. All because of him. He pushed a finger against his temple.

Regardless of the doctor's assurances that Brooke would be asleep for some time, he abhorred the idea of her waking up alone in the recovery room. Every cell in his body was telling him to go find her. He wanted to see for himself that she was okay.

Chapter Nine

Was it morning already? Brooke flinched against the pounding in her head. Why wouldn't her eyes open? She swallowed and her throat burned, the resulting cough ending in a moan.

"Take it easy, Brooke."

Why did Joel's voice sound far away?

"Chess?"

Someone took her hand and squeezed it gently. "I'm here."

She desperately wanted to open her eyes, but everything around her faded as she drifted back to sleep.

The next time Brooke woke up, she could open her eyes. Blinking at the bright lights, she squinted against the headache. Within moments, Chess's face came into view. It was blurry at first, but after blinking several times, it cleared. "Where am I?" She tried to inhale, but it felt as though something were squeezing her chest. Pain radiated into her shoulder.

"You're at the hospital. You were in a car

accident." He rubbed a thumb over the top of her hand.

"I don't remember." She started to shake her head, but the pain stopped her. "I need something to drink."

Chess moved out of view and came back with a plastic cup of water and a straw. "Take it a sip at a time."

Brooke got two swallows down before making herself stop. "Where are Joel and Anna?"

"They just left to grab some food. They should be right back. You've been in and out of consciousness for the last couple of hours." Chess set the cup back down and watched her with an expression that Brooke couldn't quite read.

"Am I going to be okay?"

"You'll be fine."

She could tell he was holding something back and fixed him with a glare she hoped meant business. "Spill it."

"You've got a concussion and a cut on your head they closed with stitches. You've also got three broken ribs."

Brooke took several shallow breaths, wincing at the pain they brought. Great. Well, the broken ribs certainly explained why it felt like an elephant was sitting on her chest. She let her eyes slide shut and tried not to worry about recovery time and what she would do about work. First, she had to get out of this hospital bed without getting sick to her stomach.

A cold hand touched her face, prompting her to open her eyes again. She found Chess studying her, his eyes filled with concern. "You really will be okay."

She gave a small nod then, her own eyes

flooding with tears. He knew her way too well. "Praise God it wasn't worse."

"Yeah."

Brooke didn't know if it was her concussion, the anesthesia from her surgery, or what. But she could hardly keep her eyes open. She could swear Chess kissed her forehead before sleep claimed her again.

"You are the most stubborn woman," Chess growled as he stuffed Brooke's things into a plastic bag the hospital had given her.

"I'm not staying at your house. You can stop asking me." Brooke shot him an icy glare.

Chess had been trying to convince her to agree to stay anywhere but her second-floor apartment by herself. The last thing she needed to do was try to maneuver up and down those stairs right after being released from the hospital. But she refused to listen. "Then take Joel and Anna up on their offer for you to stay with them."

"They're newlyweds, Chess. Absolutely not. I'll be fine. I broke a few ribs, not my leg. And I have no intention of taking anything more than the strong doses of acetaminophen they gave me." She planted her hands on her hips, daring him to contradict her. "The doctor said I was cleared to go home as long as I took it easy and rested. I can do that best in my own place."

He knew there was no point in arguing with her now. She'd made up her mind, even if he thought she was making a terrible mistake. What if something happened, and she needed help in her apartment? He pushed back the variety of situations that vied for his worry.

"I'll quit bugging you about it on two conditions."

Her eyes narrowed. "What are they?"

"You ask for Anna to come help you shower if you need it." She nodded her agreement to that and he continued. "You don't complain when I come by every day to clean your head wound and put a new bandage on it." She moved to argue, but he stopped her. She'd never been good with blood. "Are you going to be able to see it in the mirror every day without passing out?"

Instinctively, Brooke reached up and touched the gauze that covered the laceration. "I'm sure I can manage." She didn't sound at all convincing.

He stared her down.

She wrinkled her nose and frowned. "Fine." She stuck a hand out toward him.

He shook it, remembering the hours he'd spent holding that same hand while she'd slept after her surgery. It was the first time he'd ever wished he were a praying man. He'd listened to Joel and Anna pray over her at least twice during that period, not convinced it made a difference but hoping theirs would be answered all the same.

A nurse came in with a wheelchair. "Are you ready to go, honey?"

"Definitely." Brooke moved to ease herself off the hospital bed.

Without hesitating, Chess strode forward to thread an arm under hers and around her waist. He helped her get settled into the wheelchair. Brooke may act tough, but he could tell she was in a lot of pain.

The nurse turned to him. "You can pull your

vehicle up front and meet us there."

Chess gave a single nod. He collected Brooke's things and headed out the door. He drove his truck to the patient pick up area as the automatic door swung open, allowing the wheelchair passage.

Chess and the nurse got Brooke transferred to the passenger seat.

The nurse patted her shoulder. "Remember to get lots of rest when you get home, honey. I hope you heal quickly. God bless, dear."

A genuine smile graced Brooke's face. "Thank you."

The drive to her apartment was silent as Chess bit back the dozens of reasons for why he still didn't feel comfortable about her staying alone. Hearing her groan when he drove over a bump spoke of how bad of an idea it was. Anna and Joel had gone ahead to prepare the apartment before their arrival. Thankfully, he could park directly below the stairs leading to her place. "Wait a minute and let me come around to help you out."

He opened her door, took her things in one hand, and then held out the other to her. She grasped it and stepped down from the truck.

"You're making a big deal out of nothing, Chess. I'm fine." She walked ahead of him and made it up three steps before sagging against the railing.

Chess nearly dropped her things in his effort to get to her before she fell. "Your head?"

"I haven't been lightheaded since this morning. Until now, of course."

She was breathing a lot faster than he'd like, and each inhale was shallow. The last thing she needed to do right now was climb stairs.

He grunted and gently lifted her into his arms. Careful to not jostle her broken ribs, he continued up the steps.

"That wasn't necessary." She may have spoken the words, but her arms went around his neck, her hands chilly against his skin.

Before they got to the top, Joel opened the door for them. "Is she okay?"

"I'm just dizzy."

Anna was standing by the recliner. "We thought it might be good for you to stay out here where it's easier to get up if you need to."

Chess agreed and gingerly eased her into the chair. He squatted down to see her face. "Has it gotten better?"

Brooke nodded. "I'll take it easy." She pinched the bridge of her nose with her right hand.

"You nearly collapsed." She was still taking shallow breaths. "Brooke. You need to focus and breathe deeper. I know it hurts, but you heard what the doctor said about it being necessary to keep your lungs clear and make sure you don't end up with any problems. You certainly don't need a bout of pneumonia." He looked at Joel and Anna and then back at Brooke. "You can't be here tonight by yourself."

Her eyes widened and her cheeks turned pink. "You're not staying, Chess."

Anna stepped forward. "Then Joel and I will. Just for tonight, okay, Brooke?"

When Brooke peeked at Chess, he gave her a look he hoped informed her that if she didn't accept their help, it would be him. She offered a small smile to their friends. "I appreciate the offer. Thank you both. I'm sure I'll be fine tomorrow."

Chess stood again, relieved. "Good." He resisted the urge to reach over and touch her. Something he'd wanted to do constantly since she'd been hurt, as if feeling her warmth against his palm assured him she was fine. "I'll swing by tomorrow evening to help you change your bandage."

"Chess?"

"Yep."

"Thank you."

One corner of his mouth lifted. "You're welcome. Get some rest." He gave a nod to Joel, a small wave to Anna, and left.

When he got back out to his truck, he let his forehead rest against the steering wheel in relief. Brooke was home. The stress of the last twenty-four hours surged through his system, leaving him exhausted.

If that car had hit Brooke on the driver's side, or if her broken ribs had punctured a lung or worse... He couldn't finish the thought. The possibility he might have lost her yesterday made it hard to breathe.

"Pull it together." He knew she would be fine. But he'd give almost anything to be the one up there making sure she stayed that way.

It turned out to be a good thing Joel and Anna stayed at Brooke's apartment overnight, though she had no intention of telling Chess that. She'd slept in the recliner and awakened twice with nightmares that had her yelling in her sleep. One time, she woke up, and the combination of a bad headache with the pain in her ribs made her throw up. That was an agony in itself as she clutched at her ribcage and prayed for it to end. Against her better judgment, she took one of the stronger medications the surgeon had prescribed and could finally go back to sleep.

The next morning, she was feeling rough. Anna volunteered to stay with her which Joel supported completely. One of the perks of working at the restaurant she and her husband owned.

With Anna's help, Brooke took a shower and felt comfortable enough to take a much-needed nap. It was nice to get to hang out together, too. Something they hadn't done since Anna and Joel got married.

Anna handed a pint of rocky road ice cream to Brooke along with a spoon. She sat down on the couch beside her with mint chocolate chip. They relished their ice cream in silence for several minutes. Anna gave Brooke a gentle nudge. "If you need me to stay tonight, too, I will."

Brooke smiled. "I appreciate it. But I think I'll be fine. Besides, you and Joel need to be able to spend time together. I'm glad you two are happy."

"Me, too." Anna beamed. "Sometimes I think of how I ended up in Quintin and I know God led me here. The odds I'd run into Joel — into all of you — are astronomically small otherwise."

"You and Joel are lucky. I envy you both sometimes."

Anna looked contemplative. "For what it's worth, I think Chess is being an idiot."

With a frown, Brooke shrugged. "I don't know. Maybe he's the one who has common sense and I'm the one thinking like a schoolgirl with a silly crush." Except it was anything but a crush.

There was a knock at the door. Brooke glanced at the clock and saw it was almost five.

"Speaking of…" Anna stood from the couch with a wink and opened the door. "Hi, Chess."

He stepped inside, his gaze going immediately to Brooke. "Hey, girls. How's everything going today?"

Brooke exchanged glances with Anna. She would rather Chess didn't know how much of a hard time she'd had last night. "Better this afternoon." At least that was the truth. "How about you?"

"Good. I got next week off from work. Nathan will fly in for a week-long visit Saturday. He's insisting on getting a rental car and driving to the house from the airport." He set a paper bag on the counter.

Anna replaced the lid on her ice cream carton. "Wow, that's awesome. Are you excited?"

Chess slipped his hands into his pockets. "I am. Nervous, too. I don't exactly know what to expect." He shrugged. "Most of our conversations have been surface stuff. I guess we'll play it by ear. I was thinking about having a barbecue that afternoon. It may sound silly, but I'd like for you all to be there when he arrives."

Brooke was curious to meet Nathan, and she understood Chess's need for a buffer. "Of course."

Anna nodded. "I'm sure that'll be fine."

"I appreciate it."

Anna turned to Brooke. "If you change your mind about me staying, call me."

"I will. You've been a huge help but you deserve a break. Go home to your husband."

"Don't forget to take more medicine at eight."

"I won't. Promise. Thanks, Anna." She accepted the careful hug her friend gave her.

Anna put the ice cream back in the freezer and pointed at Chess. "Take good care of her."

Chess waved his goodbye and locked the front door behind her. He came back and sat on the arm of the chair opposite Brooke, his arms crossed in front of him. "I heard you had a rough night."

Brooke sighed. "Joel told you." Of course, he did. It was impossible to keep a secret in this family. She wanted to be annoyed, but she knew both guys were worried about her. "Yeah, last night wasn't much fun. But I made it and learned a valuable lesson."

"What's that?"

"Keep up with the acetaminophen." She nodded slowly and then offered him a smile, hoping to put him at ease.

He returned it, though a bit tentative. "And you're sure you don't need them to stay with you again tonight?"

She released a long-suffering sigh. "I'm sure."

Chess seemed to disagree but said nothing.

Brooke put the lid on her own carton and before she could move, Chess took it and the spoon into the kitchen. When he returned, he was all business. "You ready for me to help you change the bandage?"

"Yes, thank you. All the supplies they gave me are up there on the counter in that bag."

Chess got it and spread the items out on the coffee table. "All right, let's get this old one off first and see what we've got."

Brooke scooted to the edge of the couch and lifted her chin so Chess could see better. Compared to her ribs, Brooke hadn't thought about the head laceration as much.

Chess gingerly peeled the soiled gauze until the

cut was exposed. His eyes shifted to hers. "You alright?"

She nodded and moved a little, trying to take some of the pressure off her injured ribs. "I'm fine." The air felt cool against her wound and Brooke resisted the urge to lift her hand and touch it. "How bad is it?"

"Considering the damage to your car, I'd say you were lucky."

Brooke's brows rose, and she grimaced against the pain. "Did you go by the lot?"

He nodded and pulled his phone out. He opened the photos and gave her the device.

As she thumbed through the half dozen pictures, her throat became dry. "Wow. I had no idea it was this bad." She handed the phone back to him. "If I'd been hit any other way, or if someone had been in the passenger seat…" her voice faltered. "Praise God it wasn't any worse."

Chess put the phone away and pointed to the paper bag. "I brought back what I could find in the car. Your snow globe from Joel and Anna didn't even break." He studied her face. "You should go peek at your head in the mirror if you want to."

Curiosity got the best of her and she stood slowly. After the headaches and dizzy spells last night, she had learned to take it easy. Thankfully, any similar reaction today was minor in comparison. She made her way to the bathroom, aware that Chess was following close behind.

She cringed when she saw the laceration. It was high on her forehead, but still visible, and the whole area around it was bruised. "Well, that's going to leave an ugly scar." She frowned at the image of herself.

"You're beautiful, Brooke. The scar will only

add character."

Chess's husky voice brought her gaze up to intersect with his in the mirror. Her heart leapt to her throat.

"I'll wait for you out there." With that, Chess retreated to the living room.

She studied her reflection and took in her unruly hair and pale skin. He thought she was beautiful? His words warmed her and suddenly the wound didn't seem nearly as bad.

Chapter Ten

Chess waited for Brooke to return to the living room, taking advantage of the time to school his features and bring his emotions in check. The last thing he wanted was for her to think the scar would in any way make her less pretty. She'd always been one of the most beautiful women he'd ever met, and it certainly didn't change how he felt. However, it wasn't good he was letting his mind go down this path at all. He tried to convince himself that he might have given Anna the same compliment, but he knew that was a lie.

Brooke walked back into the room and took her seat on the couch. Chess leaned in to clean the wound like the doctor instructed them to. When that was done, he got the antibiotic ointment out. He dabbed some gently along the length of the cut, being careful not to irritate the stitches. Brooke exhaled slowly, the air brushing against his chin and neck. He fought to keep his attention on what he was doing when her eyes threatened to pull him in. Her lashes fell, shielding her brown orbs.

He placed a new bandage and fought against the urge to cover it with a kiss. "There we go." He stood abruptly. "Does it hurt?"

"Mostly when I raise my eyebrows." She demonstrated and winced. "Compared to the ribs, it's a minor annoyance."

"Do you still have your ribs wrapped?"

Brooke nodded. "Anna helped me with that earlier today. It's weird how putting tape over them can help, but it does." Her cheeks colored a little. "I'm not going to show you, but the bruise is bigger than my hand and a dark purple."

It was Chess's turn to wince. He could imagine. He cleaned up the supplies and then washed his hands in the kitchen sink. "Do you have anything easy I can get you for dinner?"

There were shadows under Brooke's eyes, and she covered a yawn. "Anna made a batch of egg salad and put it in the fridge. There's enough for both of us if you want a sandwich."

Things were still awkward between them, but he had to grasp any opportunity to try to fix their friendship. Besides, after her accident, he wasn't in a hurry to leave her alone.

He insisted she rest on the couch while he made the sandwiches, located chips in the cabinet, and a bottle of lemonade from the fridge. Before long, they were sitting side by side, their food on the coffee table in front of them. He bit into one of his sandwiches and nodded. "Excellent choice."

"They do hit the spot."

They ate in silence for a few minutes before Chess thought of something to ask her. "Did you get to talk to your boss at the salon?"

"Yes. I said I needed the next two weeks off for sure, and then I could re-evaluate." She frowned. "I can barely manage to get up and down right now, I can't fathom being on my feet for hours."

"You don't sound like you're in a hurry to go back."

Brooke shrugged. "I had two weeks of vacation I could take. Let's just say I'm looking forward to the break, though I'm not a fan of how it came about."

"Have you thought anymore about a career change?" He had a feeling she mostly didn't want to say anything. "Come on. There's got to be something. Extreme couponing? Biochemistry?"

The suggestions brought a smile to her face. "I considered one of those year-long archaeological expeditions to a far-off country might be good." She sobered. "Seriously, I have no idea and I find that completely sad."

Chess paused a moment. "Did you have any hobbies when you were young that helped keep your mind off everything in foster care?" He watched as she stared up toward the ceiling in thought, pulling that lower lip of hers between her teeth. She looked cute when she did it, but it was worrying it happened more frequently nowadays. He probably shouldered a lot of the reason for that.

She must have come up with something because she gave a little shrug and focused on her sandwich, her cheeks painted pink.

"Come on, tell me about it."

She took a long drink of lemonade. "Fine. It's silly, though. I have a limited number of clear memories of my mom." A wistful expression passed over her face. "But she's drawing in almost all of them.

I loved watching her bring something to life on a blank page and wanted to be just like her when I grew up."

Chess knew her mom had died of a stroke when Brooke was only five. An elderly relative had taken her in for two years or so until her health prevented her from continuing to care for her great niece. That's when she entered the foster care system. His heart ached for all Brooke had gone through. He waited for her to continue.

"My mama's aunt knew how much those memories meant to me. She gave me one of my mom's sketchbooks to keep and then bought me one of my own. Back then, I hoped I'd learn to draw as well as she did." Her voice broke.

He had no idea. "Did you ever draw?"

"Some. At least until I ended up in foster care. I didn't much feel like it after that, you know?"

"Yeah. I get it." It was easy to lose a little of yourself every time you moved from one foster home to another. And Brooke had mentioned she bounced around frequently until she was fifteen. That was enough to change any child. It'd certainly changed him. "What did your mom use?"

"Pastels, mostly." Brooke smiled a little. "I can still remember what they smelled like." She picked at the bread on the last few bites of her sandwich with a slender thumb and finger.

"You should take an art class at the community college. Start drawing again." But as soon as Chess said those words, she shook her head, the corners of her mouth dipping down. "What? Why not?"

"Because that's not going to pay the bills." Brooke held her arms out. "I've got to pay for this apartment. Hopefully the insurance will come through so I won't have a slew of medical bills." Her voice cracked. She cleared her throat and took another drink. "I'm probably stuck at the salon for now."

Chess hated the dejected look on her face. He was lucky enough to have a job he enjoyed for the most part. Even then, he could imagine what it would be like to feel trapped in a position that seemed unending. He wanted to do something to erase the sadness from her face. His gaze settled on her lips and the unexpected need to kiss her flooded his system with such force, it left him stunned. Without realizing it, he'd turned toward her and their faces were mere inches away. Her rose-scented shampoo floated around him as his heart threatened to beat right out of his chest.

There was a red spot on her lower lip from when she was worrying it earlier. As much as he wanted to kiss her — needed to kiss her — it would only give her hope. His actions had already resulted in her car accident and injuries. He couldn't risk it. Couldn't risk her.

He stood abruptly, covering his action by gathering their plates. "You should search through some options. You have two weeks to figure something out if you do want to leave the salon."

Brooke's gaze fell to the floor, her voice quiet as she spoke. "Maybe. But sometimes, no matter how hard we want them to, things never change."

Guilt pummeled him as he took their plates into the kitchen and washed the dishes. By the time he returned to the living room, it was a few minutes after six. He found Brooke in the recliner, her legs curled up beside her and her head resting against the back. Her chest rose and fell with each breath of a deep sleep. His heart swelled and turned over.

Chess found a blanket and spread it out over her before taking a moment to study her face. With one finger, he softly brushed some hair off her cheek, allowing himself the luxury of letting his hand linger near her ear before withdrawing it.

He would have to be more careful around Brooke. The last thing he needed to do was mess up and kiss her. Or say something he couldn't take back. He'd drawn a line in the sand before and anything else would only muddy it and make things worse.

Anna said Brooke needed to take more medicine at eight. There was no way he was leaving before then. He observed Brooke as she slept, the all too familiar waves of guilt flowing through him. No matter what, he wouldn't let her or Nathan down again if he had any control over it.

When Brooke awoke the next morning, it took her a moment to remember she'd been sleeping in the living room. She vaguely recalled waking up at some point in the evening to find Chess watching over her. He got her some more medication, helped her shift positions in the recliner, and she'd promptly fallen back to sleep.

The chair was empty now, but a note in his handwriting rested on the coffee table. She reached over to retrieve it.

Brooke,

If you get sick again at any point in the middle of the night, call me. I'm serious. Sleep peacefully and don't forget to take your medicine. Text me when you get up in the morning, okay?

Chess

Her phone was plugged into the wall on a shelf across the room. She stood slowly, relieved to find the headache had eased tremendously compared to the day before. Her ribs, however, hurt even worse than they had last night. She supposed that was probably normal, but the pain made it difficult to take full breaths like she knew she needed to.

She distracted herself by typing a text to Chess and sending it. *"Just woke up. I didn't get sick, and I feel better this morning."* Her ribs might hurt more, but her head was a lot clearer.

A reply came a minute or two later. *"I'm glad to hear that. Anna's going to come check on you at lunch and I'll be by to help with the bandage this evening. If you need anything in between, let us know. Take it easy today."*

"I will. Thank you."

"You're welcome."

Brooke found a box of chocolate donuts on the counter in the kitchen and chose one for breakfast. As she ate, she thought about her conversation with Chess last night. She hadn't considered drawing again. She had to admit the idea of taking an art class had potential. But simply because her mom had skill didn't mean she did.

She had some faded memories of her great aunt telling her she drew much like her mom. How long had it been since she'd gone through the art books from her youth?

Brooke finished breakfast, took some more

medication, and then made her way to her bedroom. Her ribs protested as she carefully pulled open one of the drawers in her dresser. Brooke knew what was inside and dreaded the flood of emotions going through the contents was sure to unleash. Even when she'd packed things up and moved into this apartment, she'd avoided looking at them too closely. This time, she prepared herself and pulled the contents out.

Inside was everything she had when she went into foster care. The art portfolio her mom loved to draw in was on top. Brooke thumbed through the pages. It'd been years since she studied the colorful images of ponds and koi, a field of Bluebonnets, and even a few portraits. Brooke's favorite was the sketch her mom did of her when she was three or four. She could still remember her mom asking her if she'd sit real still and keep stirring the cake batter for a while.

Brooke didn't mind. It meant she got to sit up on the counter, while wearing Mama's apron, and sneak little licks of chocolate batter when she thought Mama wouldn't notice.

Looking at the picture now, Brooke realized how much talent her mom had.

She closed the book and let a hand rest on the cover. There was no way she had any hope of being as good. Aside from doodling, she hadn't even drawn since she entered foster care. The realization it was almost two decades had Brooke shaking her head. So much time...

The next thing in the drawer was one of Brooke's own art books. This was the book Auntie had given her. Brooke didn't know how to use the pastels back then, but it didn't matter because she was drawing like her mama had.

Brooke remembered thinking they were amazing images. But she was certain, when she opened the book, she'd find scrawls of a child who had no idea what she was doing.

She lifted the cover and gasped. No, they weren't anywhere near as good as Mama's. But wow, they were far better than anything Brooke had expected. Had she truly drawn these? She came to the image of a little stuffed bear. Brooke rummaged in the drawer and lifted the same stuffed animal. The drawing was anything but perfect, but it wasn't half bad.

Auntie said she had talent like her mom, but Brooke hadn't been ready to hear that. Maybe it didn't mean that much then. But now...

She swiped at the tears in her eyes and released a shaky breath. She reached for the last thing in the bottom of the box. Paper towels wrapped around a set of handkerchiefs. She remembered sitting at Auntie's feet, watching her expertly use a shuttle and colorful thread to create beautiful tatted lace that bordered the squares of cloth. Brooke lifted them to her nose, amazed they still held the faint scent of lavender she'd always associated with the elderly family member who'd cared for her as long as she could.

She'd never forget the tears in Auntie's eyes when she gave Brooke a hug from the hospital bed. *"Keep your head up, Brookie. Your mama would want that. Don't forget her. Or me. Okay?"*

Brooke blinked back tears. "How could I, Auntie? I love you."

"I love you, too, my sweetheart."

A few days later, Brooke remembered when someone informed her at her foster home that her great aunt had passed away. The last connection she had to her mom was gone. It was also the day that Brooke packed everything away.

"I never forgot about either of you," she said through the tears. She squeezed her eyes shut tight. "God, give them a hug for me. Let them know I still love them."

She let herself cry for a bit and mourn what she'd lost. Something she hadn't done in a long while.

Entering foster care had been the beginning of the loneliest time in her life. Until God introduced her to Joel. And then Chess. Now Anna. A family He knew she needed more than anything else.

Her thoughts turned to Chess. He'd been so sweet and helpful last night. For the hundredth time, she wished she'd kept how she felt about him to herself. If she had, things between them wouldn't be as strange and awkward like they were now. Her heart stuttered in her chest at the memory of how close they were when he was treating her wound, and she sighed with frustration. Would she ever be able to think about him without reacting like this?

"It doesn't matter what I do, things were bound to change. I want to turn back time to when things were simpler. But I can't, can I?" Tears gone, Brooke groaned and began to pack her things away, leaving the two art books out on her bed. "Should I search for somewhere different to work? God, a little direction would be nice. I'd love to know what I'm supposed to do now."

Chapter Eleven

Brooke did her best not to flinch when the nurse approached her with a small set of scissors. The nurse snipped the first of the five stitches and used tweezers to gently tug it loose from her skin.

She hadn't realized how nervous she was until Chess placed a strong hand on her shoulder. She released the death grip she'd had on the edge of the table, her knuckles white. Even with everything going on between them, Brooke was grateful she didn't have to go to the appointment alone. She released a nervous laugh. "I'm glad I wasn't awake when you put these in."

The nurse chuckled. "They're certainly a lot easier to get out, that's for sure." She clipped the next stitch and removed it. "Three more to go. The skin is healing nicely."

Chess rubbed a calming thumb over her shoulder. The motion succeeded in taking her focus off what the nurse was doing. She concentrated on the way the heat from his hand seeped through her sleeve to warm her skin.

Once the last of the stitches had been discarded, Brooke released a sigh of relief. As far as she was concerned, the worst was over.

The nurse cleaned off the little table and threw several things away. "You can shower normally now. I still recommend putting antibiotic cream on it for another week to help as it continues to heal."

Brooke nodded, touching the area gingerly with a finger. "It's already much better. Thank you."

Chess helped her stand. Her ribs, on the other hand, still ached frequently, and she got sharp pains if she moved too much or breathed in too deeply. She'd searched for it online and apparently, it could take up to six weeks for them to heal completely. Hopefully she'd feel more improvement much sooner than that. They walked out to his truck, and he took her home.

Brooke was all too aware that Chess would no longer be by the house daily now that her stitches had been removed. She fought back the sadness as he helped her to the couch and then brought her a bottle of her favorite soda from the fridge. "You seem to be feeling a lot better today. Your cheeks have more color."

Brooke smiled her thanks. She opened the soda and took a drink as he joined her. "I do, thank you." She held up the bottle. "And thanks for this, too."

"You're welcome." He glanced at her sketchbooks on the coffee table.

She'd had them out earlier, thumbing through the images to help pass the long afternoon. It made her feel closer to Mama and Auntie. She'd meant to put those away before Chess arrived and cringed as he reached for her mom's. He flipped it open and took in the different images. "Wow, these are good. Did you draw these?"

"No, my mom did." Brooke gulped when he paused at the drawing of her stirring batter on the counter. "That's me."

He lightly touched the face of the carefree girl. "You were an adorable little girl. I see you loved to cook even back then."

"I was her shadow. I wanted to either watch or help no matter what Mama was doing. She must have had the patience of a saint." She gave a quiet laugh. Those memories were what she hoped to replicate with her own child one day.

Brooke's breath caught when he looked up at her and smiled. He motioned toward the other book. "What's that one?"

"Those are some of my drawings before I went into foster care." She knew he'd trade books and resisted the urge to grab it before he could. Her face heated up as he slowly browsed the drawings.

Chess nudged her arm with his. "These are amazing. You were what, like seven? You have a true gift."

She tried to ignore the zap of electricity at his touch. Just when she thought things were getting better in that department. "Had. It was a long time ago."

He turned his body to face her. "So?" He tapped one of the sketches. "You should draw again."

Brooke shrugged and stared down at her hand where she was picking at the hem of her shirt. Chess surprised her by gently kicking her foot with his own. The motion brought her gaze up to meet his.

"You've always been bad about representing your worth, Brooke. You are one of the kindest, smartest, most capable people I've ever known." He reached a hand toward her before bringing it back to his side. "I wish you could see yourself the way I..."

She couldn't look away from his eyes. His expression morphed from puzzled to conflicted. What was he thinking? What she didn't need was for him to see how much he'd affected her. Poor, pathetic Brooke couldn't get over the silly crush she had on the guy who was supposed to be her big brother.

Yeah, she'd never seen him that way. Not even back in the beginning. It'd been a little more like hero worship then. Now?

The way Chess was watching her made her heart hammer painfully against her ribs.

She was in love with him. Brooke knew she cared for him. But *love*? The realization only sent the butterflies careening even more madly in her belly.

What did that make her? *A pathetic mess.* Because Chess had made it clear he didn't feel that way about her. Brooke took the sketchbook from him and held it in her lap, needing a shield between them.

"Brooke." She didn't respond, and he tentatively touched her arm. "Are you okay? If I embarrassed you about your art, I didn't mean to."

Brooke shook her head. "I'm sure I'm just tired."

Chess studied her face and seemed anything but convinced. "I know things have been hard lately. I hope you still consider me a friend."

She nodded. "Of course. Friends." She tried her best to give him a normal smile, but wasn't sure she'd succeeded. "You know me. I've always messed up when it comes to guys. I can't tell you how badly I've wanted to take back what I said to you and everything could go back to the way it was before. You and I weren't all that close..." She paused, willing herself to not get emotional. "But I still miss the way we were. It was easier that way."

Chess flinched at Brooke's words. He'd always been careful to keep that boundary up between himself and her. He'd needed to. But it bothered him to know she'd had feelings for him and hadn't felt free to voice them. He didn't blame her. And when she had, he'd pushed her away. He was lucky she still spoke with him at all right now. She didn't think they were that close before, and he was the one to blame. Was he partially at fault for how insecure she was about herself? The possibility didn't sit well with him.

She might wish things were back to the way they were before. But he didn't. In fact, he felt closer to Brooke now more than ever, and he didn't want to give that up. Was that selfish? Maybe.

"I'm not good with expressing my emotions, Brooke. I was never one of those kids who wore his heart on his sleeve." He reached for her sketchbook and placed it on the coffee table. "You are one of the most important people in my life. I'm sorry if I've made you feel like that isn't true."

Brooke bit her bottom lip as tears filled her eyes.

"Don't doubt your self-worth, girl. Not ever. You hear me?" A sudden need to kiss her came out of nowhere. Chess had to quit putting himself in these positions where he was much closer to Brooke than he should be.

She nodded, and a single tear escaped to flow

down her cheek. He wanted to brush it away but instead, he stood and pulled a tissue from the box on the counter. He handed it to her and sat down again.

Brooke took it with a half-smile and dabbed at her face. "You know, this has been a few of the hardest weeks. I put my foot in my mouth and then the accident was horrible. I'm not sure what I'm going to do about another car." She appeared pensive. "I know you don't like hearing me say stuff like this. Maybe God's using these situations to push me into doing something with my future. I feel like I've been waiting around for life to begin when I'm the one who needs to make it happen." She shrugged and blushed a little.

"Brooke, that's ridiculous. You're saying God took advantage of what's going on with us and He arranged your car accident so you'd get bored enough and do something different. What kind of crappy thing is that?"

"No. That's not what I'm saying at all. What if God saw what happened and thought, 'You know, Brooke's life is gonna be shaken up. She's getting frustrated with her job and the accident means she'll have two weeks off. Maybe now's a good time to give her a little nudge in the right direction'."

She had to be kidding. Every time she or Joel would talk about how God helped them out with a situation, he wanted to knock some sense into them. "I respect your beliefs, Brooke. But you'll never be able to convince me God's up there watching over us. If He were, the three of us wouldn't have gone into foster care. You wouldn't be sitting there with broken ribs." Chess crossed his arms and raised his brows at her as though daring her to come up with an explanation.

"Let me tell you something, Chess. My mom

died when I was six. I'm not sure I'd remember much about her if Auntie hadn't taken me in and reminded me every day what my mama and I did together. It's because of that extra two years that I have more memories than I would have." She shifted on the couch, her arm briefly brushing against his. "I lived in the foster care system for most of my childhood. Miraculously, nothing bad ever happened to me. The one time it almost..." Her voice broke. "One of the boys at that home tried... Well, the foster dad caught him and made sure I was safe. And then I ended up with the Zieglers."

Hearing her words and her experience stunned Chess. That anyone had dared to try and lay a hand on Brooke like that... "I'm sorry. I had no idea."

She shook her head. "I'm not trying to make you feel bad for me. At the Zieglers, I was sure I would age out of the system alone. And that's when I met Joel." She smiled at the memory. "It was like I'd reached my limit and there he was. Right when I needed him. Instead of ending up on the streets by myself, we made it through and moved out together. I thought we'd be home free. And when we thought we'd reached the end of our ropes, God brought you into our lives."

Chess watched Brooke as she spoke. He didn't understand her faith. But sometimes he envied that she had such a strong belief in something.

Her eyes sparkled. "Things haven't been easy for me, Chess. But guess what? They could have been a whole lot worse. I'm thankful for the memories I have of my mama. I'm thankful for the time I spent with my auntie. And I can't imagine my life without you or Joel in it. That, I wholly credit to God. He watched over me the entire way and when I didn't think I could walk another step, He picked me up and carried me."

Brooke reached over and took his hand in hers, her skin warm and soft. Chess ran his thumb over her wrist, amazed at how right it felt. He should pull his hand away, but instead, his eyes traveled from their joined hands to her face.

"God used you to make a difference in Joel's life. In mine. You were there for Nathan in the beginning and now you'll have the chance to get to know the brother you lost. Think about it, Chess. You may not believe in God, but He obviously believes in you." She leaned over and placed the softest of kisses against Chess's cheek. "I'll be back in a minute." She stood slowly, one arm across her broken ribs, and left the room. If she was as conflicted as he right now, she probably needed the escape.

All Chess could do was stare at the space she'd vacated while her words seemed to echo in his head. His chest ached. He tried to push everything she'd said into the back of his mind, but it refused to obey. What she said was impossible. He'd spent his whole life assuming that, if there was a God, He didn't care one lick about him. The idea that He not only knew who Chess was, but cared what happened to him, was absurd. The hair on the back of his neck stood on end.

A knock at Brooke's front door brought Chess to his feet.

Brooke re-entered the room and went to answer the door. "Larry? What are you doing here?"

Upon hearing the guy's name, Chess moved to stand just behind her. He didn't miss the way the shorter man's eyes widened when he saw Chess.

She put one hand on the door and the other on her hip.

Larry wiped his palms off on his pants and shifted his weight from one foot to the other. "I stopped by the salon to talk to you. One of the ladies there said you had an accident and were on vacation." He looked nervously at Chess then back to Brooke. "Were you hurt?"

Chess resisted the urge to lecture the guy on his use of stalking as a way to impress a woman. Brooke wouldn't appreciate it if he interfered. She'd made that much abundantly clear in the past. She surprised him, though, when she took a little step to the side, bringing her close enough to brush Chess's arm with hers.

"I'm doing okay. I appreciate you asking, but you shouldn't be here."

Larry frowned and it was clear he hoped Chess would leave them alone. When Chess made no move to do so, Larry took a minute step back. "I just wanted to come by and see if there was anything I could do to help."

Brooke shook her head. "I don't need anything from you, Larry." The meaning behind her words was clear.

It looked like Larry might object until his gaze collided with Chess's. Larry's attention moved to Chess's belt where the outline of his holstered forty-five could be seen beneath his shirt.

Larry visibly blanched. "Right. I guess I'll be going."

He turned to leave when Brooke said, "Don't come back here, Larry."

The guy gave her a single nod, avoided Chess completely, and left.

Chess looked over at Brooke. A feeling of protectiveness toward her combined with satisfaction in knowing she wasn't going to let Larry weasel his way back into her life. "I'm proud of you."

She gave him a sad smile. "You know, I'm exhausted. If you don't mind, I'm going to try to get some rest."

"Of course." He almost said he'd see her tomorrow except that wasn't true. Now that she had the stitches out, she didn't need him to come and help her clean and bandage the cut. He choked back the disappointment.

Brooke cleared her throat. "I'll see you on Saturday for the barbecue, okay?"

"Yeah. You'll call if you need help with anything?"

"I will."

Chess fought against the mixture of disappointment and relief as he said goodbye and walked out of her apartment. He should be glad to return to normal and only see Brooke when they were all together. He ought to be relieved that he didn't have to watch what he said or did every minute he was around her.

But the only thing he felt acutely was her absence.

Chess's mind swirled with everything he and Brooke had talked about. If he'd been more open in the beginning, would she have shared about her experiences in foster care? Would he have been able to help her have more self-confidence? After everything that had happened to her, how did she have such a strong faith in God?

He finally picked up his phone and dialed Joel's

number two hours later.

"Hey, Chess. What's up?"

"I messed things up with Brooke, didn't I? No wonder she doesn't like to talk to me about the important stuff like she does you. And then, when she finally does tell me something, I make a mess of that, too."

"Where's this coming from? Did you guys fight?"

"No." It probably would've been easier if they had.

"You're taking way too much credit for the crap Brooke's gone through that fed into her insecurities. Don't forget her dad walked out on her when she was a baby. If he'd been around, she'd never have entered the foster care system in the first place." He paused. "You've been there for her since we first met you. Don't discount that. Just because your relationship with Brooke differs from the relationship she and I have, doesn't mean it's any less."

It was almost as though Joel had overheard the conversation between Chess and Brooke. Did he believe God used Chess to help them, too?

Chapter Twelve

Saturday turned out to be a hot one. Chess stood in the sun with Joel as the steaks cooked, but both Anna and Brooke chose to sit near the glass sliding door where the porch roof sheltered them from the sun. Chess hadn't spoken with Brooke since Thursday evening. He kept stealing glances at her, trying to discern whether she was doing okay. While she still favored her side a great deal, she didn't appear to be in as much pain.

Joel must have caught him watching her because he said, "Brooke's tough."

Chess nodded. "I know." But that was the problem. Sometimes she was too tough and didn't ask for help when she needed it. Chess was feeling off balance himself with too many unknowns floating around him. Between Brooke's future, their friendship, and meeting Nathan for the first time today, he struggled to shake off the unease.

The doorbell rang and the four friends looked at each other. Pushing back waves of nerves, Chess hollered, "I've got it." He hurried through the house to the front door, unlocked it, and pulled it open.

A man two or three inches shorter than Chess stood waiting. Hazel eyes he'd recognize anywhere held a mixture of uncertainty and determination. Chess had imagined this meeting a dozen different ways in the last week. Now that they were both standing here, he didn't know what to say.

Nathan shifted the bundle he held and cradled it in his left arm. The pink and purple blanket slid over to reveal the sleeping face of a baby girl. He stuck his now-free arm out. "I'm Nathan."

Chess took his hand and shook it. "Chess."

The men stared at each other for several heartbeats until Chess registered that he hadn't asked Nathan inside yet. He held the door wide open. "Come on in. My family and I are grilling in the backyard. I'll introduce you."

Nathan nodded. He carried the baby in his arms and wore a large backpack. Chess couldn't see the baby well enough to tell how old she was. Why hadn't Nathan mentioned her before now? It seemed like a child would be one of the first things you'd share. Chess led the way through the house and into the backyard. The moment Nathan stepped through the sliding glass door, he had everyone's attention. Anna and Brooke got to their feet and Anna called Epic over to her side and encouraged him to stop barking. Joel laid the spatula he was using on the little table next to the grill, dusted his hands off on his pants, and held one out.

"Hello there. I'm Joel."

Nathan shook his hand. "I'm Nathan Kirkpatrick. It's nice to meet you." He held the baby up a little. "This is my daughter, Mia."

Chess introduced Brooke and Anna, who greeted Nathan with smiles and handshakes as well.

Chess motioned to one of the patio chairs. "Feel free to have a seat."

"How old is she?" The question came from Brooke.

Nathan smiled brightly at the question. "She's five months." He gazed down lovingly at the blonde-headed baby. "She was a trooper on the flight here. She'll be waking up soon. Can I fix a bottle for her inside when she does?"

"Of course." Chess motioned to the back door. "Can I get you something to drink?"

"I'll take a Dr Pepper if you have one."

"Yep. Be right back." Chess was going inside when he heard Brooke say something and then hurry in behind him. They walked together to the kitchen.

"Wow." Brooke's eyes were wide. "Did he tell you he had a daughter?"

"Not a word." He glanced over his shoulder to make sure no one else had come into the house. "I wonder if he's married."

Brooke retrieved the soda from the fridge before Chess could. "He's not wearing a wedding ring."

That she'd noticed that fact immediately annoyed Chess. In that moment, he registered the possibility that one day, Brooke might fall for someone he knew. He'd have to go on watching her live her life and raise a family. The thought didn't sit well with him. He looked over to find her staring at him.

"There's no doubt you two are related." She held the bottle in both hands and leaned against the counter. "You guys appear a lot alike. He's not quite as…" She stopped herself, blushed noticeably, and straightened.

Nathan wasn't quite as what? Chess pinned Brooke with a stare he hoped would get her to finish her sentence. But she pressed her lips together and handed him the bottle, their fingers brushing. He reached out and lightly touched her arm. The simple gesture sent a jolt of electricity straight to his heart. Chess did his best to ignore his reaction. Nathan was only one reminder of how he'd failed in keeping family safe before, and why he had to protect Brooke by not letting his emotions take over. He studied her eyes, hoping for some hint about where they stood. "Are we okay?"

Brooke gave him a little shrug. "Things are different, Chess."

"I know." He'd never wanted this uneasiness between them. He wished he had the time to sit down and talk to her right now. Though he had no idea what he would say.

"I'd better get back out there." She gave him a sad little smile and retreated to the backyard.

The moment she stepped away, the surrounding air cooled and the kitchen felt empty. Chess followed her outside and passed the soda to Nathan.

"Thanks." Despite the baby in his arms, he managed to twist the top off and take a swig. "I hope I'm not intruding."

Joel returned from flipping the steaks again. "Not at all. We've been looking forward to meeting you since Chess told us about your visit." He pointed at the grill. "We have plenty of food and hope you'll stay for dinner."

"I appreciate that." Relief marched across Nathan's features followed by something else Chess didn't quite catch. The baby stirred and her little eyelids fluttered open. Nathan smiled widely. "Hey, girly. We're finally here." He glanced up. "She didn't sleep a wink on the plane. The moment I got her into the rental car, she crashed."

Mia rubbed at her eyes and blinked up at her dad. He shifted her until she was sitting on his lap. Wide, blue eyes took in all the strangers around her.

Nathan rubbed her messy hair into some semblance of control. Several spots popped back up again. He chuckled. "She's way more outgoing than I am. But she takes a little while to wake up. I'm going to run in and fix that bottle if it's okay."

"Absolutely." Chess moved to open the sliding door as Nathan bent over and dug around in his backpack for a bottle and some formula.

To Chess's surprise, Brooke stood. "I'd be happy to watch Mia for you if she'd let me."

Nathan seemed uncertain and looked down at his young daughter. "Do you want to stay here with Miss…" He looked at Brooke. "I'm sorry. Remind me of your name again, please."

"Brooke."

"… with Miss Brooke?"

The baby's gaze swung to Brooke before she buried her face in her daddy's shirt.

Nathan nuzzled his daughter's head. "Don't take it personally."

Chess almost joked that it reminded him of Brooke. She wasn't nearly as bad about it now, but years ago, she balked at getting up early. When she lived at the house, she often nursed a cup of tea in the morning for at least twenty minutes before he or Joel even dared to start up a conversation.

He missed having her around every day.

Chess shook off the thought. "Here, I'll show you to the kitchen."

Brooke watched the guys return. As soon as Nathan settled back into the chair, he handed the bottle to Mia who snuggled into her daddy's arms. She started drinking hungrily, her gaze ever vigilant and curious.

The baby brought a smile to Brooke's face. "She's adorable. I love those long eyelashes." Everything about the baby was fair compared to Nathan, from the light skin to the blonde hair to the blue eyes. She looked nothing like him except for her nose. That was a miniature version of Nathan's. And Chess's, too, for that matter.

"Thank you." Nathan kissed the baby's head. "She's a sweetheart." He surveyed the small group. "So how do you all know Chess?"

Chess exchanged a glance with Brooke and she gave him a little nod of encouragement. "Maybe I should start at the beginning."

Nathan listened, his eyes on his daughter. He didn't say a word as Chess repeated everything he'd told Brooke and the others. About how Nathan had been removed from the foster home despite Chess's attempts to stop them.

Nathan frowned. "I was told by my parents — my then foster parents — that they wanted to adopt us both but you said no. And that's why you stayed behind. As I grew up, they avoided answering any questions I had about you or the time I spent in foster care. I always wondered why."

Chess shook his head. "I don't know why they would tell you that. A caseworker told me the foster family couldn't keep you because you were too young and you were going to a more appropriate home. I promise, nothing was said to me about adoption."

The actions of Nathan's adoptive parents stunned Brooke. All she could figure was they thought Nathan would best move forward if he left everything about his past behind. Memories of her mama and great aunt, no matter how painful, meant a lot to her. She couldn't imagine being denied even those.

"Yeah." Nathan used one finger to caress the back of his daughter's hand. "Well, I'm certain growing up with my adoptive parents was better than the foster care system. But they had a lot of their own issues. They got a divorce when I was ten and pretty much live separate lives even now. I bounced back and forth between them until I was eighteen and I see them once a year at most." He paused. "With all the lies they told each other, I shouldn't be surprised they'd lied to me from the very beginning. They probably thought they were protecting me." He cringed. "I wish I could've remembered more for myself."

Brooke's heart ached for Nathan. When she was a kid, she'd imagined all would be solved if someone would choose to adopt her. As if it would be a magical ending to a nightmare she couldn't wake up from. But this was proof not even that guaranteed a lifetime of happiness.

"It's understandable. You were so young."

Chess's voice sounded strained. He recounted his story about how he'd searched for Nathan all through his childhood.

Brooke still didn't like that Chess had kept his past, his little brother, a secret for as long as he did. But if she'd spent a big chunk of her life hunting for a long-lost sibling and never knowing what happened to him... Well, it was hard to know what she'd do. She caught Chess's gaze and gave him what she hoped was a supportive smile.

One corner of his mouth came up but fell back down again. "You know that day at the food bank when I met you and Joel? That's when I finally let go of my obsession to find Nathan."

Mia finished her bottle. Nathan took it from her, set it on the patio at his feet, and rubbed circles on the baby's back. He seemed to be deep in thought.

Anna leaned over to whisper in Joel's ear. He put an arm around her and drew her closer. "I told you about how Brooke and I met at the same foster home and then left together once we had both aged out of the system." Anna nodded. "We rented a horrible apartment, but we couldn't make enough money to keep it. After a while, we were staying on the streets or anywhere we were able. We went to a local food bank once a week for the food that kept us going. That's where we met Chess."

Brooke took over the story from there. "I noticed him a couple weeks in a row." She blushed, realizing that she'd admitted something she'd never told Chess before. "Then, one week, he overheard us talking. We had gotten eggs and milk from the food bank. But since we were living on the streets, we had no place cool to keep it. We were about to give them away to someone who could use them before they went bad when Chess came up to talk to us. Eventually, he invited us to stay at his apartment for a few days until we could get back on our feet." She'd never forgotten that day, or what it meant. It was a new beginning and it changed her life. Hers and Joel's.

Chess paced to the edge of the concrete patio before coming back and sitting down again. He looked at Nathan. "I went to that place once a week. But it wasn't because I needed the food. I hoped that, somehow, I'd run into you. I frequented several food banks in town along with the shelters." He paused and turned his attention to Joel and Brooke. "I heard you two talking and decided I was spending my life in the past. I did my best to move on from there. Part of that, for me, was not talking about it." His gaze connected with Brooke's.

"Chess…" But Brooke couldn't say more. There were a lot of things that happened between them, but she hoped he knew she wasn't upset with him for not telling them about Nathan and his past back then. "I get it." She also understood now why he jumped at the chance to move them all to this house in Quintin a couple of years later. There were too many old memories in Dallas.

Nathan looked thoughtful. Mia bounced up and down on his lap and he brought the baby to his chest and patted her back. "You're all lucky you found each other the way you did." He glanced up at Anna. "How about you?"

Joel took her hand in his. "She joined the band earlier this year. We were married a few weeks ago."

Anna leaned into his shoulder.

Nathan smiled, but it seemed sad. He kissed his

daughter on the top of her head. "That's wonderful. Congratulations."

"Thank you." Joel stood. "I'd better go check on those steaks. How do you like yours, Nathan?"

"Medium well, please. If you're sure it won't be an imposition."

"Not at all."

Brooke knew the steaks would be close to done. She exchanged a look with Anna. "Maybe we should go get everything else ready."

Anna stood quickly and seemed relieved. "That's a good idea."

They went through the sliding glass door and Brooke turned to close it behind them. Chess watched her through the glass with concern. She wanted to tell him everything was going to be okay, but, how could she? She prayed finding Nathan again would help Chess put some of the past behind him.

Chapter Thirteen

Chess watched Brooke and Anna go into the house, Epic on their heels. He wondered what they were talking about. With Joel checking on the steaks, it was just him, Nathan, and Mia sitting under the covered patio.

He focused on Nathan. "I'm sorry your childhood was rough. It couldn't have been easy to see your adoptive parents fight like that."

Nathan took his daughter's hands and helped her stand on his lap. She grinned and happily hopped up and down. "Well, I didn't make it easy on them, either. I guess I was a troublemaker. I got into a lot of fights in school. Sometimes I wonder if I wasn't a big source of the issues between my parents though they assured me that wasn't the case." He took in a deep breath. "I'd be a real mess now if it hadn't been for one of my teachers. I tried to deck him when I was sixteen." Nathan's ears grew red at the memory. "But instead of sending me to the principal where I'd be suspended, he convinced my dad to enroll me in Brazilian jiu-jitsu. It was the best thing anyone did for me." Mia flopped back down on her bottom and waved at her daddy. He smiled and waved back. "Turns out, I had a lot of anger I needed to work out. And doing that in a constructive, safe environment probably kept me out of jail later."

Chess nodded. "I'm glad you had that." Wow, their lives had been completely different. He wondered if Nathan even knew what happened to their biological parents. Chess had worked to put that behind him and thought today may not be the time to bring it up again. "Do you still practice it?"

"I do. I'm a black belt and an instructor back in Florida." Nathan seemed proud of his accomplishment.

Chess knew little about jiu-jitsu but imagined it took a lot of dedication to reach that level. "That's awesome." Mia smiled at him. Where was the baby's mother?

"Do you want to hold her?" Nathan held Mia out to him. "I'll bet she'd like to say hi to her uncle."

Chess blinked at the baby. He was an uncle. She was his niece. The thought seemed foreign. He took Mia and gingerly set her on his knee. Thank goodness, the girl was old enough so Chess didn't worry about having to support her head or anything. Even still, she seemed tiny in his hands. She clapped her own together and offered him another smile punctuated by a bit of drool that dribbled off her chin and onto her shirt.

"Sorry. She's teething, though I've yet to see a tooth break through." Nathan withdrew a handkerchief from a pocket and leaned over to wipe off his daughter's chin.

Chess caught Joel watching them from the grill.

He offered a smile of encouragement before rejoining them.

"Steaks are about ready," Joel announced.

Nathan stood. "I should probably change her diaper before dinner. Where's your restroom?"

Chess gave him directions and handed the baby back to her daddy. The duo went inside. Joel approached, carrying the platter of steaks. "Are you doing okay?"

Chess had no idea how to answer that, and Joel seemed to understand. He pointed at the house. "You should invite them to stay in Brooke's old room while they're here. It'll give you two a chance to catch up."

"Yeah, that might work." He looked through the sliding glass door at Brooke and Anna busy in the kitchen. Brooke was laughing at something and her face lit up. It was good to see her smiling like that again. She'd been way too serious the past couple of weeks.

Once inside, everyone gathered around the table for the meal. After several moments of eating in silence, Nathan nodded toward his plate. "This is fantastic. Thank you for inviting us to join you."

"You're welcome." Chess had a list of questions he wanted to ask Nathan and had prioritized them. He started with one of the easiest. "So, you live in Miami now?"

He nodded. "Yes. We have an apartment there." He shifted Mia from one leg to the other, balancing her as he ate.

"Are your adoptive parents in the area?"

Nathan frowned. "No. Once they split, I guess they needed to get as far apart as they could. My father lives in Montana and my mother up near Maine. Even when I see them once a year at Christmas, it's at different times."

"I'm sorry to hear that."

"It is what it is. I appreciate it though." Nathan looked around the table. "You have a great family here."

Chess's gaze collided with Brooke's. Her cheeks colored slightly, and she dipped her chin, focusing on her plate. "Yeah, I do. We're lucky we found each other." He watched as Brooke peeked at him again. Sure, both she and Joel were family. They were everything to him. But it was then that Chess realized Brooke meant home. He shook the thoughts from his head and brought his focus back to Nathan.

His brother must have thought the silence was because of him. He finished his bite of food and set his fork down. "I know you're probably wondering about Mia's mother." He paused. "Gwen isn't in the picture." Nathan cleared his throat. "Our relationship was less than stable when we found out Mia was on the way. Shortly after Mia was born, Gwen said she hadn't signed on to be a mother. She gave away all rights and disappeared."

Nathan grimaced. Chess felt sorry for him and the baby. He remembered what it was like to watch their mother check out of reality in her own way and how hard it'd been. Maybe it was a good thing that Mia didn't have to witness that herself though she would surely grow up wondering why her mother had left. "I'm sorry to hear that."

Nathan kissed the top of his daughter's head. "Gwen and I made a lot of mistakes, but I'll never see Mia as one of them. We're happy. Aren't we, girlie?" He blew raspberries against the baby's arm and she rewarded him with a belly laugh.

By the time Brooke finished her meal, she was absolutely stuffed. It was getting on towards evening and her ribs were aching from all the moving around. She sat and listened to everyone else visit, her mind wandering. It was hard to see the others move forward in a way. There was Joel and Anna, happily married and going home together tonight. Now Chess had his biological brother back in his life with a niece as icing on the cake.

Where was she? Feeling a bit like the third wheel when it came to either party. She realized it was mostly her problem, and she was certain none of the others felt the same way. But it was still difficult to shake.

A wave of loneliness flowed through her. She was relieved when Joel and Anna said they were about ready to leave. Brooke had caught a ride with them and welcomed the excuse to go home as well.

She shifted positions, holding back a grimace when her ribs protested. "It was wonderful to meet you, Nathan." She reached over and gently held Mia's hand. "And you, too, little miss. I look forward to seeing you both again."

She turned and went in search of her bag. Brooke had closed the front door behind her and began to follow her friends when the door opened again, and Chess jogged down the steps to meet her.

"You don't have to leave, Brooke. Come back inside and stick around for a while. I can take you home later."

She was shaking her head before he was done.

"I don't think so. You guys should have some time to visit by yourselves. You finally found your brother. I'm happy for you." She truly was, but her emotions were waging a war inside her. It was silly, but she was feeling more than a little sorry for herself. She glanced back at Joel and Anna who were already seated in the car waiting for her. "You've got to stop following me out to my car." She meant it as a joke, but it fell flat. "I'm going to go home and relax. Besides, my side's bothering me tonight. Go and get to know your real family."

Chess's expression hardened, and he gave her one of his exasperated glares. "I know what you're thinking, Brooke. You are my family." He paused at his own words and shoved his hands into his pockets. "You, Joel, and Anna and you know it. Nathan and Mia would be an addition to that. Don't make me feel guilty because I found my biological brother."

Brooke's shoulders fell, and she closed her eyes slowly before opening them and taking in the wounded expression on his face. "You're right. That wasn't fair." She wanted to leave it at that and escape to the car. But he was watching her in a way that always somehow coaxed her thoughts out of her head. Sometimes it was completely annoying. "I'm grumpy and I'm hurting. But that was no excuse. I'm sorry." Ants had built up some red dirt in a crack in the driveway, and Brooke ran the toe of her shoe along the trail.

Chess moved closer, his shoes inches from hers. "Tell me what's actually going on."

He was close enough for her to catch a whiff of his aftershave. "I guess I'm unsure of where I fit in the whole grand scheme of things. Joel has Anna. You have Nathan and Mia. Everyone's changing. But where am I? In the same place I've been since I was nineteen. I realize it's childish, but I can't help but feel that way." Her confession resulted in warmth climbing her neck and flooding her cheeks.

"You still have Joel." Chess's gaze bore into her. "You have me. That will never change."

"Let's face it, Chess. You can't be sure of that."

To her surprise, he gently put his hands on her shoulders and bent until they were face to face. "I'm sure because I won't let it change."

His words were low and a little husky. They sent a shiver down Brooke's spine, bringing goosebumps to her arms. What she desperately wanted was for Chess to pull her into a hug. She wanted to listen to the beat of his heart, feel his chest rise and fall with each breath, and have his protective arms holding her close. *That's what I want, God. Preferably forever. Is that too much to ask?*

As if he'd heard her thoughts, Chess took a small step back. He searched her face for several moments before he broke eye contact. He cleared his throat. "I should probably get back in there."

Brooke nodded.

"I'll check on you tomorrow."

She bobbed her head again and watched as he hesitated and then went back inside. The air whooshed out of her lungs. Her legs wobbled as she walked the rest of the way to the car.

"Are you okay?" Joel examined her in the rearview mirror.

"Not really." It didn't matter how hard she fought the sting of tears, one still escaped. She brushed it away. "Why does this have to be so hard?"

Anna got out of the car and moved to the back

seat where she could reach over and give Brooke a hug. "I don't know. I'm sorry you're hurting right now."

Joel started the engine and drove to Brooke's apartment building. They parked, but no one moved to get out.

Brooke sniffed and groaned. "I'm tired of crying and trying to act like everything's okay. It feels like every time Chess and I make progress, something happens and we take two steps back again." She rested her head on the back of the seat and closed her eyes. "With everything that's happened, maybe we're destined to drift apart. What if it's better that way."

Joel shifted. When she opened her eyes, he was looking back at them, an arm hooked over the top of the driver's seat. "Chess is stubborn. He gets too caught up in thinking he has to protect everyone, sometimes to the extreme."

"You think?"

Joel tapped her knee to get her attention. "He's got a lot on his plate right now. He needs to sort through everything with Nathan. And how he feels about you."

"He's made how he feels perfectly clear, Joel. That's the problem." Brooke let her head fall back and closed her eyes. "I'm in love with someone who doesn't feel even a hint of the same for me." She didn't miss the look that passed between husband and wife. "What?"

Anna gently nudged Brooke's right arm. "I think he loves you, and he's not ready to admit it to himself."

Brooke had a real hard time believing that. "Well, he sure has a messed-up way of showing it."

Joel frowned. "Don't give up on him. A lot is

shifting for Chess right now. Sometimes we're unwilling to see things differently until we're no longer comfortable in our lives."

"Did I tell you I had the opportunity to share a little about our faith with him last week?" As Brooke relayed the conversation, the pain in her heart ebbed a little. When she was done, Joel and Anna both appeared hopeful.

"It's more than we've been able to do since we've known him," Joel said with a smile.

Anna nodded. "Then we keep praying for him."

They all talked a little longer and by the time Brooke entered her apartment, she was feeling better. She took some medication, re-bandaged her cut, and went to bed. She fell asleep easily and dreamed about cooking with Mama.

Chapter Fourteen

Sunday evening, Chess's mind continuously traveled back to the conversation he had with Brooke after the barbecue the day before. She'd looked lonesome and it'd taken every ounce of his strength to let her go.

When there was space between them, he knew keeping an emotional distance was the right thing. In the end, Brooke would realize that, too. Because one day, she'd meet a guy who could give her everything she wanted from the white picket fence to the house full of kids.

But in those moments when he was close enough to inhale her fragrance or touch her, a part of him wanted to do whatever it took to make things work between them. The thought of anyone else holding her was something he couldn't even entertain. It seemed, no matter what he did, his heart was in constant conflict with his head.

He'd promised Brooke he would check on her today and it was getting late. Steeling himself and putting his emotions aside, he closed his bedroom door and called her.

"Hey, Chess."

"Hey yourself. Is your side feeling better than it was last night?"

Brooke moved something around in the background. "A little. How are you guys? Are Nathan and Mia settling in okay?"

"Yeah, they seem to be fine. I'm not sure what we'll do tomorrow, but I thought I'd take them to DFW for a while." He paused. "We'd talked last week about my picking you up and taking you to get groceries on Tuesday. I'd still like to help if you'll let me." There was no sound on the other side of the connection and Chess checked to make sure the call hadn't been severed. "Brooke?"

"Things are getting pretty thin around here. I'd appreciate your help."

"Good. I'll come by and pick you up at ten in the morning if that works."

"Sounds great." She was silent again for a few moments. "Hey, Chess? I'm glad you are reunited with Nathan. You're a good brother, and he's lucky to have you."

Chess sat on the edge of his bed and let himself fall backward across the mattress. "I don't know about that, but I appreciate it. Sleep well. I'll talk to you soon."

"Okay. Bye, Chess."

"Good night, Brooke."

He hung up and stared at the ceiling. Hearing Brooke's words, combined with the fact that Nathan didn't seem to hate him for not being there when he grew up, made his heart lighter than it had been in a long time.

The next morning, Chess awoke to his alarm clock like he normally did. Even in September, it was still dark at five. It wasn't until he'd stood and stretched that he remembered he didn't have to drive in to work. He'd arranged to have the entire week off so he'd have time to visit with Nathan. It'd been a while since he'd taken such a long vacation. He decided it was way overdue.

He could go back to sleep, but there was no way that would happen now. He listened for any indication someone else was awake in the house and didn't hear a peep.

Chess took a shower, went through his e-mail, and then made his way to the kitchen to pour himself a glass of orange juice. He took a sip and wrinkled his nose at the strange combination of tastes between the juice and the toothpaste he'd used. Nathan walked into the room just as Chess got himself a bowl of cereal. Chess raised a spoon in greeting. "Good morning."

"Morning." Nathan grabbed another bowl and joined him.

"I hope you guys are comfortable in there. If there's anything else you need, let me know."

"We're good. Mia slept straight through the night, which she doesn't always do at home, if that tells you something."

Nathan had brought in a portable crib to set up in Brooke's old room where they were staying.

"I'm glad to hear that."

They ate in silence for a while before Nathan set his spoon in his bowl, his expression serious. "I have a confession to make."

Chess paused mid-bite. His little brother

certainly had his undivided attention. "Oh?" He tried for nonchalant and had no idea if he was succeeding.

"I'd like to move up here. Outside my job, I have nothing waiting for me back in Miami. I even spoke to my instructor about it and got recommendations for two Brazilian jiu-jitsu academies in the Fort Worth area where I could apply for work." Nathan sat up straighter. "I wanted to come up here and meet you first, see how you felt about the possibility. Truthfully, I have everything packed and a moving company scheduled to bring my stuff a week from today unless I call them tomorrow evening and cancel."

Chess's eyes widened. He still didn't know Nathan well, but the idea of having his brother and niece living nearby held a lot of appeal. It had to have taken a lot of courage to fly all the way up here hoping things worked out the way Nathan had planned.

He nodded slowly. "I was hoping I could take you and Mia into the Dallas area and introduce you to the city. We can scope out those academies and see what kinds of apartments or houses there are for you to rent."

Nathan's face transformed into a bright smile. "Does that mean you have no objections to my relocating here?"

"None. I'll be glad to have you nearby, little brother."

Brooke held her grocery list in her left hand as she marked another item off. At least she was being useful since Chess insisted on pushing the basket and gathering almost everything off the shelves. It was sweet, though. It took little for her ribs to cause her pain, and she was grateful for the help. She glanced over at Chess when he tossed a box of cereal into the shopping basket and looked at her expectantly. "What's next?"

Still, it would've been less awkward if she could've gone shopping by herself. Of course, there was the small issue of not having a vehicle to drive. She frowned.

"Did I get the wrong kind?" Chess retrieved the cereal and double checked the front.

"No, that's the right one. Thank you." Okay, she needed to quit wallowing. Regardless of how weird it was between them, Chess was doing her a big favor by taking her grocery shopping. It couldn't be any easier for him. "Canned fruit is next."

Now it was Chess's turn to frown. "Stay here, and I'll be right back."

She watched as he jogged down the aisle and out of sight. She doodled on the paper, drawing a likeness of the basket and its contents. Five minutes later he returned triumphant and held a box up for her to see.

"An electric can opener?"

"Yep. Now you won't have to strain yourself opening the cans. One bad twist and those ribs won't heal as quickly." He set the box in the basket. Before she even had time to object, he put his hands back on the handle of the shopping cart and pushed it. "And I'm buying it for you."

Ugh. He knew her too well. She was trying to conserve money and purchasing an electric can opener, no matter what it cost, wasn't a necessity. But she knew better than to argue with him when he took that tone. "I appreciate it." Suddenly, a memory from the first year they were all together came to mind, and she chuckled. "Do you remember when you bought that fancy vacuum cleaner?"

Chess tipped his head back with a laugh. "You and I argued for a week about why we should or shouldn't buy it."

"I thought it was frivolous. We had that little one that still worked."

He looked at her in mock seriousness. "If you want to call making enough noise to wake the dead and emptying the canister every five minutes working."

She grinned. "When you brought that new one home, I was furious."

"Until I showed you how it worked for the first time." He raised an eyebrow.

"When I got done vacuuming in a third of the time, I finally had to concede you were right. I didn't feel bad when we threw the other one away." Her gaze rested on the electric can opener. Even back then, Chess was buying or doing things that helped to make her life a little easier.

He startled her when he tapped a finger against her grocery list. "That's incredible. I'm serious, you're good at this."

She studied the doodle of the shopping basket and absently hit the end of her pen against the shopping cart.

They turned onto the canned fruit aisle, and she was thankful for the distraction. They continued shopping for a half hour before Chess spoke. "Nathan's going to move here."

"Really? That's great." Brooke dropped her

pen and before she had the chance, he got it for her and handed it back. "When?"

"We went to Fort Worth yesterday. His instructor in Miami had given him a referral to someone who owns an academy there. We stopped by, and he has an interview with them tomorrow along with another appointment at an apartment complex. I'll be watching Mia all day while he goes to those."

"Wow! That's fast." She picked out several apples and placed them in the plastic bag Chess was holding for her. "How do you feel about it all?"

"Well, it turns out he'd packed everything up hoping this would work out. Movers are bringing his things by on Monday." Chess twirled the bag, put a tie on it, and set the apples in the basket. "I'm glad he's moving here. He says he won't be leaving anything but his job. I got the sense he was sad about that. I guess this instructor took him under his wing when he was a kid."

Brooke was happy he'd not only found the brother he'd been searching for, but that Nathan and Mia would be moving locally. Funny how this time last year, it was just her, Joel, and Chess. Now there were six in their little group. Seven if you counted Epic.

Maybe that's what Brooke needed — a pet. The idea had some merit. After her ribs healed, and she had a vehicle again, she might seriously consider it.

She focused on what they were doing and found Chess watching her closely. "Are you getting tired?"

"A little. Mostly I'm zoning."

"Let's get this finished up, and I can take you home. What else do you need?"

She double checked the list. "Bell peppers,

bananas, and then bread and we'll be done."

With a nod, he headed for the peppers. A moment later, he shot her a teasing grin. "I could move stuff around and you can ride in the basket if you get too tired."

"Not in a million years." She reached for a plastic bag and handed it to him. When he tried to get it, she moved it away at the last minute.

Chess raised an eyebrow. "Don't make me tackle an injured woman in the middle of the produce section." His eyes dared her to keep at it.

Brooke's face warmed from her neck all the way to the top of her head. She'd been trying to keep the lighter mood going but now worried he thought she was flirting with him. Even worse, maybe she was.

She moved the bag within his reach and his hand grasped hers to hold it still. The familiar tendrils of energy made their way down her arm and into her bloodstream. Her pulse skyrocketed and no matter how much she wanted to turn away, his gaze kept her rooted.

Chess took a step closer, and then another, never letting her hand go. With his other, he took the plastic bag. The corners of his mouth quirked. "Good choice." He released her hand and moved away.

Completely shaken, Brooke forced herself to focus. "I'll go get the bread." She walked the short distance to the bakery and let her eyes slide shut, attempting to regain some composure. It was then she realized it would always be this way when she was around Chess. No matter how well her brain understood their relationship, her traitor of a heart would refuse to give up hope. It would always react to him when he was near because she couldn't imagine not loving him.

She would have to put physical distance between them. She thought about Nathan searching for apartments in Fort Worth. Perhaps she should do something similar. It would still be close enough to attend weekly family meals, but far enough to give her the separation to think straight.

Brooke had started doing research online when a basket approached. Grabbing a loaf of bread and schooling her features, she turned and placed it in the seat next to the bananas. "I think we're done. Let's get out of here."

Chess gave her a questioning look, but she buried her sadness and led the way to the checkout lines. She desperately needed fresh air and a little space.

Chapter Fifteen

Nathan was around long enough the next morning to get Mia changed, dressed, and a bottle made before he took the rental car and headed for Fort Worth. Chess was left holding his niece in his arms. With wide eyes, she stared at him and stuffed a fist in her mouth.

"I guess this will give us a chance to get to know each other a little." Mia looked from him back to the door where her daddy had disappeared. "How about you drink that milk and I'll make myself some toast?"

He handed the bottle to Mia, and she began to cry. Her distress only increased when Chess tried to get her to take the bottle, offered some of the applesauce Nathan had left, and eventually walked with her around the house.

An hour later, she finally drank most of her bottle. But it didn't seem to quell what bothered her because moments later, she was crying again. He might go deaf, which could be a blessing given the circumstances.

By nine, he decided they needed to get out of the house for a while. Nathan had moved the car seat over to Chess's truck before he left. Chess packed supplies, got Mia buckled in, and headed out to do some errands. The moment the truck was moving, Mia quieted down. If they had to stay on the go all day, then that's exactly what he'd do. By ten-thirty, at least Mia had stopped reacting to him as though he were a scary gargoyle, and he even coaxed some giggles if he acted silly enough.

Back in the truck, he started the engine to get the air conditioner going and dialed Brooke's number. She answered on the third ring. "Hello?"

The sound of her voice caused his pulse to stutter. He immediately thought back to their shopping trip the previous day. He pictured the way she'd looked at him in the produce section, amusement and something else he didn't want to analyze lighting up her face. Holding her hand, he'd wanted her to keep teasing him with the plastic bag so he could...

What? Have an excuse to hold her? Kiss her?

Should it bother him that he might have done all that if she hadn't relinquished the bag?

"Chess?"

He shook the thoughts from his head with a groan. "Hey, Brooke. I'm out doing some errands with Mia. I have something I want to drop by, and we're about to pick up lunch. Can we bring you something?"

She didn't respond right away and Chess wondered if she was as affected by their closeness the day before. If so, maybe she needed an out. Maybe he did. "You know, I can get this to you this weekend, it's not a big deal." Mia started to fuss now that she was strapped in and the truck wasn't going anywhere. He put the vehicle in drive and slowly made his way across the parking lot. That seemed to appease his niece, and the crying ceased.

"No, it's fine. Come on by."

He swung through one of Brooke's favorite Chinese food places on his way to her apartment. She had the door open by the time he'd climbed the steps with Mia in his arms, the backpack that served as her diaper bag, plus the bag of takeout in his hands.

"Whoa. Let me grab something." Brooke took the food and closed the door behind him. "What all have you guys been doing?"

Mia swung her head from side to side, probably searching for Nathan. She put a hand in her mouth and began to cry.

Chess set the backpack on the coffee table and moved to pat Mia's back. "We've been on the go since nine because if we stop, she cries like this."

Brooke stroked the baby's hair. "What did your Uncle Chess do to you?"

He gave her a disparaging look. "Oh, you know. Terrible things like try to feed her, make her smile, and walk ten miles around the house before surrendering."

Brooke placed a kiss against Mia's silky hair. "I'll bet you're missing your daddy, aren't you? He'll be back in a few hours. Trust me, hanging with your uncle is probably a lot more fun than sitting through an interview and meeting. If you stop crying, you'll feel a lot better. Your eyes won't hurt as much and your poor nose won't be as runny." She got a tissue and wiped the baby's nose before she realized Chess was watching her. "What?"

"Reasoning with her. Why didn't I think of that?" The corners of his mouth twitched as he tried to keep his face serious. She gave his shoulder a shove, and he grinned.

"Whatever." She nodded toward the Chinese food. "Good choice, it smells amazing. How about I fix a bottle for her quick?"

"That'd be great. There should be some applesauce in there, too. Though I had a horrible time getting her to eat anything at breakfast."

Chess walked Mia around the small living area. Brooke's voice floated in from the kitchen. "Have you tried music?"

"What?"

She peeked her head around the corner. "Try putting on some music and see if that helps distract her."

That wasn't a bad idea. Chess took his phone out and found one of the local country music stations online. A song came on, and Mia stopped crying and reached for the phone. "Oh, you like that, huh?" Chess turned the sound up and set the phone on the counter. "I'll have to tell your daddy you like country music. A sure sign moving to Texas is the right thing." He chuckled.

Chess could barely hear Brooke singing along in the kitchen. He'd always enjoyed listening to her sing. She may not have a recording voice, but it was clear and sweet. She stopped as she came into the living area with the bottle.

"Here we go." She handed it to Mia who began drinking it hungrily. Brooke smoothed her hair back and smiled when Mia reached for her. Brooke held her close and swayed a little with the music.

Chess studied her and how easily she interacted with Mia. She was a natural with children. He could suddenly picture Brooke holding her own baby with dark hair and chocolate eyes like her mother. Beautiful. He swallowed hard, pushing the vision he had no right picturing out of his head. Desperate to redirect his attention, he tilted his head toward the phone. "You're a genius."

"I wouldn't go that far." Her cheeks turned a pretty shade of pink. "Music makes everyone feel better."

"I'll go grab the food." He brought the bag and unpacked the cartons, arranging them on the coffee table. Brooke nodded her approval when she saw orange chicken.

"Give me that girl before you hurt your ribs, and have a seat." Chess traded her a plastic fork for his niece. He bounced Mia on one knee while he ate his broccoli beef.

They chatted about the weather and something funny that Anna had told Brooke.

Chess's attention was drawn to the little dab of sauce on the corner of Brooke's mouth. He had to fight to not reach over and use his thumb to wipe it away. Were her lips as soft as they appeared? Thoughts of kissing her came to mind before he knew what was happening. It seemed like every time he was around her, the need to do just that became harder and harder to ignore.

Brooke was watching him as though she were waiting for him to respond. He must've been staring at her mouth hard enough to miss something she said. His ears got hot, and he jerked his gaze from her to his meal. "Sorry, what was that?"

"I was asking if you were enjoying the time off from work."

"It has been nice. It's going by way too quickly, though." They both fell silent.

It amazed Chess how fast they'd gone from being comfortable around each other to the thick awkwardness that surrounded them now. How was he supposed to act? She was right about what she said the other day. It was a lot easier before everything changed. But the more he thought about it, the more he realized he didn't want to go back to the way things were. At least she'd told him about her parents and he'd shared about his childhood. He knew a lot more about her now than he ever had before.

The truth was, he'd been closing *himself* off from everyone because he wanted to leave the past behind. In reality, by doing that, he was really shutting *them* out. Wow, he'd been clueless.

Most of this wouldn't have been possible if it hadn't been for Brooke's vehicle breaking down, her accident, and Nathan reaching out to him. He thought about what Brooke said. *"Maybe God's using these situations to push me into actually doing something with my future."* He wondered how likely it was the same thing was happening to him.

"You may not believe in God, but He obviously believes in you."

Brooke's words repeated themselves in his head. He'd been wrong about a lot lately. What if he was wrong about God, too? What if what Brooke said was true? Chess had not only ignored God all his life, but sometimes purposefully rejected the idea that He existed at all. He couldn't blame God if He chose to dismiss Chess after everything.

How could God believe in him when all Chess did was mess things up?

They finished eating in silence and Brooke sensed something had changed. They'd been conversing easily until Chess shut down, and she didn't understand why. Confused, she gathered their trash and stuffed it back into the plastic bag before carting it to her trash can.

She got back to find Chess on the floor wrangling the squirmy baby into a new diaper without much trouble.

Chess caught her expression and laughed loudly. Mia jumped at the sound and stared at him with wide eyes. "You seem surprised I know how to change a diaper."

"I never pegged you as a baby guy."

His eyes were unfocused as his expression sobered. "I took care of Nathan most of the time when he was an infant. Then one of my foster homes had a set of twins who were toddlers. You think this is bad wait until Mia's running around." He sat her on the floor and kept a hand against her back to keep her from toppling over. "She's close to being able to sit on her own."

"She sure is." Brooke watched the baby reach for the container of wipes. For the first time in a long while, she'd thought about her dad walking out on her when she was little. Mia's mom had done the exact same thing. She prayed this little one would grow up realizing what an amazing job her daddy did at keeping things together. Hopefully living near Chess would give her the family she could depend on growing up. She realized Chess was watching her, concerned.

He kept supporting Mia with his hand, but all his attention was on Brooke. "What were you thinking about?"

She shrugged, hoping he would let that be enough. But she could tell by his expression it wasn't. "My father. He left when I was a little younger than Mia. I don't know if he ever played with me or held me. I'll never know if I made him smile or if he rocked me until I stopped crying. Or why I wasn't enough." Tears were building again. She'd cried more these three weeks than she had most of her life put together. It was getting ridiculous. She cleared her throat and forced the tears back. "I realize it's dumb. Mia isn't me, but I can't help but envy her support system. She's lucky to have a dad who will do anything for her and you for an uncle."

"Your mom sounds like a great lady from what you've said. Even if you don't remember it, I'm sure she reassured you many times that your dad leaving had nothing to do with you. It likely had nothing to do with your mom, either, and it was all him."

Brooke didn't remember Mama talking about him at all but she was sure Chess was right. All Mama ever did was take care of her, nurture her, and make her feel safe. "Yeah. I know."

Chess rummaged through the diaper bag. "I almost forgot we brought you something." He withdrew a plastic bag and handed it to her. "I did some research and hopefully got the right things."

She stared at it, almost afraid of what might be inside.

Chess shot her a bemused smile. "I didn't coil

up a viper and stick it in there, if that's what you're wondering. Just open it."

Brooke chuckled nervously then carefully withdrew the contents. She ran a finger over the new sketchbook and then opened the pastels, breathing in their scent. Tears pricked the back of her eyelids. "I don't know what to say."

"You have talent. I remember seeing the little doodles you'd make on the phone pad or when you'd write notes on that whiteboard we used to keep by the front door. Those weren't the ordinary doodles Joel or I might have drawn. I never thought about it back then though. I guess I had no idea." He gently allowed his shoulder to bump into hers. "You deserve to focus on something you enjoy. You don't ever have to show me anything you draw, but if you want to, I'd like to see them."

"This was sweet. Thanks, Chess."

She felt the warmth of his arm against hers. There were a hundred reasons for why she should move and create some distance, both emotionally and physically. But right now, she couldn't have moved if she tried. She willed her runaway heartbeat to slow down. Could he hear the way it was pounding inside her chest?

"Any time." Chess's voice sounded gruffer than usual, and he cleared his throat. "I still think you should take some art classes."

Brooke's smile faded a little. "I'm thinking about it. Maybe in the spring. Things are on hold until I figure out what I'm going to do about a car and all that. I go back to work next week, too."

"You don't sound thrilled. Are you still considering a potential change of professions?"

Brooke shrugged. "I don't know. I'm praying about it. There's an opening at the bookstore at one of the community colleges in Dallas. Maybe if I worked there, I'd get a discount on classes. Or at least I'd be close enough to take one a semester."

The stricken expression on Chess's face said he'd never considered the possibility she might try to find something outside Quintin. "If all of that came together, would you move?"

Soon, Chess would have his biological brother and niece in the area permanently. If she chose to move and put some distance between them, she wouldn't be leaving him alone. "It'd probably make more sense." How could she tell him that it'd be easier on her to not see him as often? Maybe then she'd have a shot of moving past whatever this was between them. The pain in his eyes made her feel even worse. "It's all up in the air. I want to get through Monday first."

"Yeah." Mia squealed and Chess picked her up. "We'd probably better get out of your hair and let you rest. Anna and Joel are having everyone over to their house for dinner on Saturday. Are you going to be there?"

"I wouldn't miss it. Besides, I'm bringing dessert."

His smile appeared forced. "Good. We'll come by and pick you up on the way. I guess I'll see you then."

She watched them leave and moved a hand to gently finger the delicate roses growing on the potted bush nearby. When he'd originally given her the bush, she'd thought it was a symbol of the hope she had that he'd one day see her as more than a little sister. Now it only mocked her and her childish fantasies. She went back inside and squeezed her eyes shut as her shoulders fell.

Brooke sank onto the couch and reached for the art supplies Chess had brought her. She opened the book to the first page, withdrew a pink pastel stick, and stared at the white paper. How to begin? For some reason, this was different than simply doodling on the corner of a notepad. As if the sketchbook held higher expectations.

She took in a steadying breath and caught a hint of Chess's aftershave. He might not be alone if she left town, but Brooke already felt the loss just thinking about the possibility.

If God was working things out, it sure would be nice to be clued in on the plan.

Chapter Sixteen

Chess walked into Joel's diner Friday afternoon. He shook the rain off his jacket as thunder echoed in the distance. He'd been thinking about several things since he'd seen Brooke and he needed to talk to someone. Joel noticed him and waved, holding up a finger to let him know he'd be right over.

Chess slid into a corner booth, glad this was one of the least busy times of the day. Minutes later, Joel set a chocolate milkshake on the table in front of Chess and sat down with a vanilla one of his own. He used the straw to stir it around before taking a sip. "Don't get me wrong, I'm glad you came by. But something tells me you have something on your mind."

Joel was right, but it didn't mean it was easy for Chess to get the words out. He focused on his milkshake for a few minutes, trying to parse through his jumbled thoughts. "Brooke seems to think, even though I never believed in God, He's still somehow using me to help other people. She insists He's using her accident to nudge her toward doing something different with her life." He paused, and Joel only sat there watching him, waiting for more. "She thinks God used me to help you two back in the day and Nathan and Mia now. That doesn't make sense. Let's say God is up there and He's been watching me all this time. If I don't want to have anything to do with Him, wouldn't it make more sense for Him to focus His energies on someone else?"

Joel leaned forward, his arms resting on the table between them. "If Mia started crying in the middle of the night and Nathan wasn't there, would you go in and see what was wrong? Or crank up the tunes in your room and hope it drowned out the noise?"

"I'd go check on her, of course."

"Okay. And if Brooke called you tonight and said she needed you to go over there to help her with an emergency? You'd do that, right?"

"Yeah. What's your point, Joel?" Chess was getting impatient with this line of questioning. He didn't see how it had anything to do with his own ponderings.

"What if Nathan had called you a few weeks ago, had a situation and needed you to go down to Florida to help him? Would you? Even though it meant missing work?"

Chess had to think about that one. But eventually he nodded. "I guess I would."

"You'd be willing to do all of that for your friends. For your niece. For the brother you barely know." Joel pointed a finger at Chess. "You are one of God's *children*. He loves you. Because you don't talk to Him doesn't mean He's forgotten you or ignoring you. No matter what you do or don't do, you are *always* worth the trouble to Him. And He's forever hoping, one day, you might find your way to Him." Joel must've sensed Chess needed time to think. "I'll go help Anastasia with some inventory. If you need to talk, you know where to find me."

Chess watched him walk away. He absentmindedly moved his cup in circles on the table.

"I have no idea what to say to You." Great, now he was talking to himself. Thankfully no one else was nearby to hear him. Goosebumps appeared on his arms and the hair on the back of his neck stood on end. "I guess I'm used to doing everything on my own. I'm not sure how great of a job I've done. I don't suppose You'd like to give me a hint of what's coming?" He paused, feeling ridiculous. "The quiet type, huh? I guess I can respect that."

It was late Saturday afternoon and Chess drove a car full of people to Joel and Anna's house. Brooke was sitting in the passenger seat while Nathan and Mia rode in the back of the cab. The little girl babbled in her car seat as she and her daddy conversed about something.

Brooke had said little, and Chess was keenly aware of her discomfort. The drive felt like it took much longer than it should have.

Anna greeted them at the door and the delectable smell of chicken parmesan welcomed them the moment they stepped inside.

"Wow. It smells amazing in here." Nathan released Mia to Anna's waiting arms. "Chess is always telling me about the incredible food you and Brooke cook up."

Anna grinned. "I think it's more of a lack of cooking skills the guys possess." She winked playfully at Joel who was standing nearby. "Tonight's dinner is Brooke's recipe."

Joel shook Chess and Nathan's hands and gave Brooke a hug. "We're glad to see you guys. Come on in and make yourselves comfortable."

Twenty minutes later, they were all seated around the table eating chicken parmesan, garlic bread, and salad.

"This is great." Nathan pointed a fork at his plate.

Brooke smiled. "We used to make it at least once a week for a long time."

Chess watched as she took a bite of her own and nodded approvingly. It'd always been one of his favorites. Eating it brought back memories of when things were simpler.

Conversation flowed around the table. Nathan told them a little about Florida. "I've been teaching jiu-jitsu for almost two years now. I heard from the place in Fort Worth and I got the job as an instructor there." He beamed. "My first day is a week from Monday."

Everyone congratulated him on the new position. "So, will you live here or move closer?" The question came from Anna.

"I've rented an apartment a few blocks from work. My stuff, including my car, should arrive on Monday."

Chess nodded. "An hour and a half to drive from here to there isn't bad occasionally. But I wouldn't recommend it on a daily basis. It'll be good for you guys to be closer." He chuckled. "And his apartment is on the bottom floor. Should be a lot easier than it was to move everything into yours, Brooke." He gave her a playful wink.

She rolled her eyes. "Boy, that's the truth. I'll never live on the second floor again."

Chess watched as Nathan held a tiny spoonful of applesauce in front of Mia. She opened her mouth wide and gobbled it right up. He was proud of Nathan and the dedication he had to his daughter. There was an immense satisfaction seeing Nathan was nothing like their father.

When they finished the meal, Joel and Anna said they'd clean up and insisted everyone else sit and visit. Chess carried a full trash bag outside. Once back in, he found Brooke and Nathan sitting on the floor with Mia lying on her back between them.

Brooke reached down and held Mia's hand. She looked up at Nathan. "I think you'll like Fort Worth. There's a lot to do there." She started telling him about her favorite restaurants and stores. "We have some great malls in the area, too."

Nathan smiled at her. "Well, it'll take me a while to get used to living in a different city. I barely remember Texas. The Dallas/Fort Worth area is a little overwhelming."

"It can be. But start off getting to know Fort Worth and go from there. There are a lot of smaller communities within the metroplex."

Chess stood in the doorway and listened as Nathan made a comment that had Brooke laughing hard. Mia reached for Brooke and she helped the baby sit on her lap. The way the three of them were interacting seemed effortless.

Chess frowned. On one hand, it was great to

see his brother getting along so well with the rest of his family. At the same time, it was painful to see how at ease Brooke was with Nathan when she no longer acted that way with Chess.

What if the two of them hit it off? Mia certainly seemed comfortable with Brooke. What if Brooke and Nathan ended up dating?

Chess shoved his hands into his pockets and scowled.

Brooke noticed him, concern on her face. She stood slowly and excused herself, saying she was going to let Epic outside.

That left Chess, Nathan, and Mia in the living room. They talked for a bit, but when there was still no sign of Brooke, Chess began to worry about her. "Do you mind if I go check on something quick?"

"Not at all. I should probably change this munchkin's diaper, anyway." Nathan kissed his daughter's cheek. "You have a great family, Chess. You're a lucky guy." He stood, got supplies, and headed for the bathroom.

Yeah, he was. Chess made his way to the back door and looked outside. Epic was wandering around in the grass while a line of dark clouds in the distance sparked with lightning. He found Brooke sitting on one of the patio chairs, her sketchbook on her lap. She was focusing on her creation, green pastel stick in hand, while she sucked on her bottom lip. She didn't seem to notice him until his shadow fell on the paper.

Brooke jumped a little, dropping the pastel onto the grass at her feet. With a sigh, she leaned down to retrieve it.

Chess lowered himself into a nearby chair and smiled at her. "You always do that, you know."

"Do what? Drop stuff?" She slipped the stick back into the box and closed the top.

"No. Chew on your bottom lip when you're either concentrating or nervous."

"Well, it's been a long time since I've drawn anything. I'm trying to remember how."

She was about to close the sketch pad when Chess leaned over and stopped her by putting a hand on the page. "May I see it?" Reluctantly, she handed it to him. "This is fantastic. It's like you took the best aspects of Epic and combined them into one picture."

She studied the image. Epic was lying on green grass, a tennis ball at his feet. He was staring off to the side at something he found interesting. Epic's mouth was open, his tongue lolling, as though he were laughing. She glanced from the serene picture to the one of Epic running across the yard to pounce on a stick and drag it across the ground. She chuckled. "Yeah, I guess I did. He's such a mess."

"I'm glad you're drawing again."

"Thanks for the supplies. And the encouragement." She offered him a shy smile. "You know, I was looking around online. There are places where people hire artists to create book covers or story illustrations. Who knows, maybe I'll try my hand at something like that."

Chess studied her with admiration. "I think that's a great idea. I have no doubt people would pay you for your work." He gently nudged her arm with his elbow. "You never know. A year from now, I might be able to brag about being friends with the famous Brooke Pierce." They both laughed, but he couldn't ignore the hollowed-out place in his chest. He was glad she had plans for her future, and she deserved nothing but success. Yet there was no denying each step she took would lead her further away from him.

Brooke sat on the back patio with Chess and watched the storm front that steadily moved closer. The air smelled like rain and even felt damp. "They announced on the radio we'll probably get thunderstorms tonight and all day tomorrow. Hopefully they don't turn too severe."

"I hope not, too. We could use the rain though."

Brooke nodded. She glanced over as Chess turned the sketch pad and flipped through the three other images she'd drawn. He stopped when he came to an image of a rose and she flinched. That wasn't a picture she'd wanted him to see. Even now, she could still feel the raw pain that'd torn at her chest when she'd drawn it.

Just like the roses on the bush he'd given her, this one was creamy white with light pink highlighting the outer edge of each petal. One lone drop of water dripped from it.

Chess pointed to the drop. "Is this from rain or a tear?"

She shrugged and reached for the book, closing it again and placing it on her lap. Would it make a difference to him if she said the rose was mourning the loss of things that could never be?

He cast a sideways glance at her. "I've been thinking a lot about what you said last week. About how God can still use me to help others even when I'm not sure I believe He exists at all. You and Joel were both originally raised in homes where you were taught about God. How do I know He'd be willing to look past all the stuff I've done?"

His question surprised her and she thought a moment. "Just because I'm a Christian and my mom and aunt were, too, doesn't mean I didn't make a lot of mistakes. I got angry at God many times through my childhood. I even refused to speak to Him when I was in my early teens. I renewed my relationship with Him after I was taken in by the Zieglers and that's when I realized I was the one who ran away from Him. It wasn't the other way around. All that time, He was waiting there with open arms, hoping I'd come running back to Him one day." She raised a brow at him. "I'm anything but perfect. You of all people should know that."

He chuckled but grew serious again. "How do I know where to find Him?"

"You talk like God's gone away or something." Brooke licked her dry lips. Simply being able to have this kind of conversation with Chess was an answer to prayer. *Please give me the words You want me to say.* "Sometimes it feels like that. I know I've reached points in my life where I've taken everything for granted. I have shelter, food, clothing, and family. It's easy to forget God's there when things are going my way. Then something bad happens, and I don't see God where I think He should be." She paused. "That's how I felt after my accident. I wondered why He didn't have me leave the house a couple minutes later, or make the guy see the red light in time. It's easy to start freaking out, worrying He's left us to fend for ourselves. When all along He's right there, a breath away."

She twisted some hair around a finger and then turned a little in her chair toward Chess. "I could blame God for the car accident and all the ways it might have been avoided. Or I could praise Him that I wasn't killed, and I'll recover from all my injuries. I can be thankful there was no one sitting in the passenger seat that night." Brooke resisted the urge to reach out and touch him. "You don't have to find him, Chess. All you have to do is look up and you'll see He's been there all along."

"It would be a lot easier if we could see the whole picture." Chess stared out at the grass. Lightning jumped from one cloud to another and the green blades blew back and forth, completely at the mercy of the wind that kicked up in the last minute or two.

"It would." Brooke clutched her sketch book and pastels to her. "It'd be easier, but then where would the adventure be?"

Chess turned toward her, a small smile lighting up his face. "True." A gust of wind came through and the first large raindrops fell, creating dark patterns on the concrete slab. "We'd better get inside before this starts coming down and we get soaked."

Back inside, they enjoyed the banana pudding Brooke made and brought over. The whole time, she continued to pray God was somehow working in Chess's mind and heart, drawing Chess to Him.

Chapter Seventeen

Chess sat in his truck below Brooke's apartment on Monday, trying to decide whether he should go see her as planned, or turn around and go home. The box of pastels Brooke dropped on the floorboard of his truck now sat in the passenger seat. They must have fallen out of her bag when he drove her home last night. If she wasn't missing them yet, she would be soon.

His mind made up, he reached for those and the other items he'd seen at the store this morning. Even though he wasn't sure he should've bought them for Brooke, they'd screamed her name and he couldn't resist.

Determined to squash his nerves, he took the steps two at a time and knocked on her door. She answered moments later, her hair pulled back into a ponytail and flour dusting one of her cheeks.

Chess bit back a smile. "I'm sorry if I'm interrupting." His gaze darted to her apartment and back to her face. "Can I come in for a minute?"

She seemed surprised but stepped to the side allowing him to enter. Her apartment smelled of chicken and chocolate: an interesting combination. He handed her the box of pastels. "I found these by the front door at Joel's last night. I figured you might need them."

Brooke's eyes widened. "I didn't realize they'd fallen out of my bag. Thank you so much." She took them and set them on the counter. "I haven't had time to draw anything today. Are you back at work?"

"I took another couple of days off. We're between projects, so it was a good time to use some of the vacation I'd saved up." Chess noted the mixing bowls on the counter in the kitchen. "What are you making?"

She dusted her hands off on her pants. "I'm mixing up a batch of chocolate banana bread right now. And I'm throwing together a chicken enchilada casserole to take to Nathan the day after tomorrow, that way he doesn't have to cook the first day or two he's at his new place."

Chess tried to ignore the immediate pang of jealousy at the thought of Brooke cooking for his brother. There was nothing wrong with it and something he knew she'd do for any of them, too. She was thoughtful that way. He nodded and forced a smile. "I'm sure he'll appreciate it. He's already mentioned how much he's enjoying the authentic Mexican food around here."

Brooke flashed him a grin.

He remembered the other items he'd brought. "I saw these at the store this morning when I stopped to get a few things, and I couldn't pass them up."

She held a hand out, and he gave her the expert

level adult coloring book and a box of colored pencils. He tapped the title of the book. "I looked through this and apparently, it's designed for artists who might want to get more detailed when they color. I thought it might be a good way to relax or clear your mind."

Brooke thumbed through the pages, the corners of her mouth pulling upward. "This is neat, Chess. Thanks."

"You bet."

He watched as Brooke took a couple of steps to lay the book and pencils on the counter. "Aren't you going to go help Nathan unload the truck at his apartment this afternoon?"

"We're not sure when the truck will arrive. He's supposed to text me. I'll head that way in an hour or so, anyway." Chess's attention was again drawn to the flour on her cheeks and the way a few tendrils of hair had escaped the pony tail and hung in wisps on either side of her face.

"What?" Her voice was squeaky as she put one hand on her face self-consciously.

Chess chuckled and reached for a towel that was hanging up just inside the kitchen. "You've got flour right here." He gently used the fabric to brush the white particles from her smooth skin.

When he finished, she didn't step back, and he didn't want to move, either. He ought to give them the space he knew they probably needed. But then she lifted her chin and looked at him. He could drown in those gorgeous eyes.

"Chess…"

His lips found hers in a kiss that launched his pulse into a gallop. One of his hands cupped the back of her neck while his other arm went around her waist.

He tightened his hold on her, breathing in her scent and memorizing everything about the way she felt in his arms. What began as a gentle kiss turned to one filled with desperation and tenderness, a strange combination born of emotions that had been buried for far too long. With her hands clasped behind his neck, it made him want all the things he knew he couldn't have. Shouldn't have. Especially with Brooke.

Life was too unstable. What if something happened to his job, and she'd be forced to work to help support their family? What if she grew to resent that about him like his own mother had his father? The thought of failing Brooke in any way shattered the bubble of perfection that had momentarily cradled them both.

He broke the kiss and placed another on her forehead. "I'm sorry."

"No." She lifted her chin and her eyes snapped open. "Don't you dare, Chess." Tears filled those brown orbs, creating molten pools of chocolate. She shook her head in disbelief.

"Brooke."

"No." She pushed away from him and spun. She placed her palms on the counter and leaned into it. "I told you what I want. You know I need forever. A family." She spun around, her brows drawn together in a mix of hurt and anger. "You said you couldn't give that to me. But I've seen you around Mia. You're amazing with her. You'd be an incredible father. I can't help but wonder…" Her eyes drifted shut, her face contorting in pain. "I can't help but wonder if it's specifically me you don't want."

164

Brooke felt as though her heart were shattering into a million pieces, pain radiating in every direction. It'd been bad enough before. But when they kissed... It'd given her that brief glimpse into what forever could be like. And she'd clung to the hope that Chess was finally in the same place. She should've known better than to give her heart to him. Except that it was too late because it'd been all his for far too long.

Chess gently gripped her upper arms. "No. It's not you. I wish..." He swallowed hard.

"Wish what?" *Please. Please tell me you love me and I'm not alone in this.* She prayed he'd talk to her. Tell her how he was feeling.

A band of emotions marched their way across Chess's face. It was defeat that finally lingered. His hands slid down to hers. He held them, squeezing almost too tightly. When he gazed into her eyes, there was no mistaking the sadness and determination there.

Brooke jerked her hands from his. The air surrounding them felt as cold and empty as the space in her chest. Blood rushed in her ears. Loneliness settled over her heart like an icy blanket. "You need to go."

"What?" Chess walked around her until he could see her face. "I don't want to leave like this."

"*I* need *you* to go."

He reached for her arm, but she took a step back.

"Brooke. Please stop so we can talk about this."

"Talking gets us nowhere. I'm done trying." Half blinded by tears, she flung her door open and motioned for him to leave. All she knew was that she needed him out now before she suffocated. He hesitated but finally jogged down the stairs, got into his truck, and drove away.

Brooke stood there for several minutes, tears streaming down her face, until she finally swiped them away. Grief gave way to anger as she stared at the rose bush Chess had given her.

The five white and pink blooms mocked her as they bobbed in the wind. She clenched her teeth and reached for the nearest rose. She tore it from the branch in one motion and threw it over the side of her tiny balcony. The other four followed soon after until the bush was bare.

That bush had been one of the sweetest things he'd ever given her. And she'd allowed herself to hope even then that it meant more than friendship.

She'd been fooling herself. How long had she wasted time waiting for Chess to truly see her? He said it wasn't that he didn't want her, but how was she supposed to believe that? She replayed the kiss in her mind. Even now, as angry and hurt as she was, the memory of his lips on hers triggered an involuntary shiver.

What if that kiss hadn't meant the same to Chess? What if, after pulling away, he felt nothing for her?

Her shoulders slumped. Maybe, after everything, she wasn't enough for Chess.

Billowy clouds threatened to make good on the weather station's promise for more rain over the next forty-eight hours and perfectly matched her storm of emotions. Defeated, Brooke turned her back on the pathetic rose bush and went inside.

Every time Chess was nearby, she had to fight

against the pull of her heart. It'd be easier to learn to live without it if she could get some physical distance. Joel and Anna were supposed to come by in a few hours to take her car shopping. By tomorrow, she'd be independent again and free to take steps toward moving forward with her life.

Brooke gave Anna and Joel both a hug back in her apartment later that evening. "I appreciate you guys going with me to find a car. I'm relieved to be mobile again." She smiled at her friends and tried to ignore the headache that had developed over the last couple of hours. Combine that with her tired eyes from crying after Chess left, and she was a mess.

Twice they'd asked her what was wrong, but she didn't want to talk about it. Couldn't, or she'd fall apart again.

Joel motioned to the laptop screen on the kitchen table. The apartment listings Brooke had been browsing were clearly displayed. "Did you find anything?"

Brooke cringed. This wasn't exactly the way she'd thought to break the news to them. She shrugged. "A few that might work."

Anna read one of the listings. "In Dallas?"

"Yeah." What else could she say? She hadn't even tried to find one in Quintin.

"Is that what you genuinely want to do?" It was clear by Joel's expression he knew quite well it was all about putting distance between herself and Chess.

Was it horrible that she wasn't even feeling sad right now? She'd run the gamut of emotions lately. The tears had run out, and she was trying to think logically.

"It is. I can make it to our family dinners every week. I'll only be a phone call away." Her voice caught. "I need to do this for me."

Anna put an arm around her and gave her a hug. "We get it. We want to make sure you know none of us are leaving you behind."

Brooke smiled at her kind words. "I know. But I need to find something to work toward. I don't want to stay where I am forever." She reached out for their hands. "You are the brother and sister I never had and always wanted. I won't be far. I'll be there for your anniversaries. I wouldn't miss a holiday. And I'll spoil my nieces and nephews rotten." At those last words, Anna's face turned pink. Both Brooke and Joel chuckled and gave her a hug. "I'm serious. You guys can't get rid of me that easily."

Joel gave her a small nod. "I'm proud of you."

Anna motioned to the computer. "Come on, show us what you've found. Maybe we can help you narrow down the choices."

As they made fun of some listings and put stars next to others, Brooke laughed harder than she had in a while.

Kissing Brooke had been a huge mistake. But even as the thought registered, he knew he'd been no more capable of walking away at that moment than he would be of clearing the sky of clouds right now. It didn't matter though. One moment of weakness on his part, and he'd ruined what little of their friendship remained.

Worried about her, he finally convinced himself to try to call her later that evening. When she never answered, he headed over to Joel and Anna's house.

Joel opened the door on the second knock, his expression guarded. "Chess. What's up?"

"Have you heard from Brooke? She won't answer her phone." Even if she'd answered, he had no idea what he would've said.

Joel shot him an accusing look. "We went car hunting this evening, and we took her home." He ushered Chess inside. "She refused to talk about what was bothering her, but it was clear it was something big."

Chess took in Joel's defensive stance and the way Anna stood against the doorway, her arms crossed and her jaw set. They weren't happy with him. Well, they could join the club in which Chess was a founding member.

Joel put a hand on the back of his neck. "What happened, Chess?"

The last thing Chess wanted to do was verbalize the events earlier that day. He threw Anna a hesitant look, and she nodded, leaving the room so he could talk to Joel. "I messed everything up. Probably for good."

Joel moved to the side so Chess could enter the house. "What did you do?"

"I kissed her."

Joel's eyes widened. "And then?"

"I apologized."

Joel sucked in a breath, and it was clear he imagined exactly how everything had gone.

Chess paced across the room and back again.

"I know. You don't have to tell me anything because I've beaten myself up over it a hundred times. I need to talk to her. Make sure she's okay."

"And if you talk to her, are you going to change your mind about the two of you being together?"

Chess's head warred with his heart and eventually won. "No."

"Then let her be. It's the best thing you can do for her right now." Joel motioned to the living room and they both sat down.

Joel waited for Chess to say something and when he didn't, Joel finally spoke up. "What's holding you back? Is it Brooke?"

Chess shook his head. "I promised myself I would never get married or have a family and risk the possibility of putting them through what my parents did to Nathan and me. I have a stable job now, but what if things change? What if I become unemployed or hurt and I can't work to support her? I've let Nathan and Brooke down so many times. I need to keep things together."

"Chess, we're not guaranteed anything in this world. Nothing is a given, not employment or weather, our homes, or even our lives. What happened to you and Nathan is on your parents and on the social workers for letting you guys fall through the cracks." Joel pointed a finger at him. "You are nothing like your father. And Brooke sure deserves more credit than you're giving her, too. You can blame an unstable economy, or the alignment of the stars, or anything else you think will make you feel better. But the truth of the matter is, you're trying to swim while shouldering a responsibility that's too heavy for you and not even yours to bear. You're going to keep treading water until you find a way to release that baggage."

How was he supposed to do that? Joel could talk all he wanted to, but Chess couldn't stand the thought of failing Brooke.

"I'm not sure that I can."

"Are you in love with her?"

Even before he had to ponder the question, his heart leapt with the answer. "Yes."

"Then you'll find a way or you'll have to let her go."

Chapter Eighteen

Chess beat himself up all the way to Nathan's apartment the next day. He slammed his palm against the driver's door. What he needed was some good physical work to help distract him. But the movers who brought the truck said they had to be the ones to unload everything due to company policy. Instead, they waited until the movers had done just that, and then Chess helped Nathan rearrange the furniture in the new apartment.

An hour later, Chess buried all thoughts of Brooke as he and Nathan maneuvered the couch against the far wall of the living area as Mia watched. Nathan had the genius idea of setting up the portable crib to give Mia a place to play and not get under foot. She spent most of the time watching them walk back and forth while chewing on some toys.

Nathan moved a box to a stack in the kitchen and stopped to tickle Mia's tummy. "She's being such a trooper while we're doing this."

Chess watched Nathan move several more

before he stopped and raised an eyebrow. Chess shrugged. "I'm just making sure you do it right."

Nathan shoved him good-naturedly. "Right."

Chess nodded toward Mia as she flung a toy against the side of her play yard. "You used to do that to me all the time." Nathan seemed confused, so he elaborated. "You might have been a little older than Mia. But we had a set of wooden blocks you liked to play with. Sometimes I'd build towers, and you'd knock them down. But your favorite game was to grab a block I was using to build with and chuck it as far as your little arms could throw. You'd laugh hysterically watching me retrieve it making it impossible to get frustrated with you."

"That sounds like something I would've done." Nathan's smile faded a little. "I wish I remembered you more. I think I recall something about an orange swing you'd push me in."

"It was at the first foster home we went to. You were almost three, and you'd never seen a swing before."

Nathan's brows rose. "I've taken Mia to the park. I take it our parents never did." He picked Mia up and the three of them settled on the couch.

Chess shook his head. "I'd only been to the park once or twice before you were born. We stayed at the house. I don't even think our mother brought us grocery shopping with her. I took care of you until we got into foster care."

Nathan's jaw dropped. "You were what? Five?"

"Yep. I changed your diapers, fed you. Our mother had pretty much checked out by then and it was up to me to keep you safe. You know, I always felt bad she was never there for you. I think she always had a lot of difficulties, but I remember her playing with me and laughing when I was little. More of an impression of it now than specific memories. And I wish you had those, too."

"I remember you tickling me and laughing until I couldn't breathe. And there was a kid who stole my ball. You tackled him and got it back for me." Nathan chuckled at the thought. "I have those memories, Chess. They're with you, instead of our parents." He paused. "You stood in that gap for me back then. As my brother, you did more for me than even you probably realize."

Unshed tears pricked the back of Chess's eyelids, and he swallowed past the lump in his throat. "I didn't want things to happen the way they did. It nearly killed me when they took you away." He stopped and cleared his throat. "I didn't know if you were okay or if someone was taking care of you. You were all I had. When you were born, you may not have come into a stable family. But you made my life a lot brighter because I finally had someone to talk to and spend time with." A tear escaped the corner of his eye and he brushed it away. "I look back and I think we saved each other. I searched for you for so long. I'm sorry I never found you."

Nathan was staring at the floor. "I wish I'd known and had a way to contact you earlier. I was young..." He paused. "I didn't fully understand what happened, but I grew up knowing you'd been there. But it was more like a distant memory or a fading dream. I had nothing I could really grasp."

"It wasn't your fault. It wasn't mine." Chess blinked rapidly, forcing the rest of the tears back. "I know your adoptive parents don't get along and you don't see them much. But did you have a happy childhood?"

Nathan smiled. "I did. They weren't perfect, but I went to parks and had playdates. They were there for every one of my school programs. Things degenerated as I got older, but yeah. It was a good childhood."

Chess clapped his brother on the shoulder. "I'm real glad of that." It was all he'd longed for growing up. That no matter where Nathan was, he was happy and being taken care of. That he grew up in a more stable environment than Chess had. *Thank you, God, for watching over him when I couldn't.* He felt a little silly praying like that. What were the odds God even recognized his voice? An overwhelming peace flooded him. For the first time, Chess thought about his past without the heavy regret that usually accompanied the memories.

Nathan lifted Mia into the air and whooshed her back down again, making her laugh. "We have more boxes to move and it's getting late." He set Mia down in the play yard and handed her a toy.

With the baby settled, they resumed shifting furniture around.

Nathan spoke over his shoulder. "If you don't mind my asking, what's up with you and Brooke?"

Chess nearly dropped the box he was carrying. He looked at Nathan, trying to determine the meaning behind the question. "Why? Are you interested in her?"

Nathan guffawed. "No. But I can tell you are. So, what's holding you back from asking her out?"

"Brother, you just asked a question that could take hours to answer."

Nathan grinned at him. "I'm not going anywhere." He sat on the arm of his couch for emphasis.

Chess considered dismissing the question, but Nathan's expression was open, and Chess finally told his brother about the reasons behind his decision.

At one point, Nathan stared at him with an open mouth. "Hold on, let me see if I've got this right. You've turned down a gorgeous woman who obviously loves you because of me? That's a lot of responsibility to pile on my shoulders considering I've only known you all for a little over a week."

Chess rolled his eyes. "Not because of you. But because I can't seem to protect the people I care about the most. I was supposed to be there for you and look what happened? I watched our father as he flung insult after insult at our mother. Little by little, everything she was faded away until only a shell of her was left behind." He swallowed hard. "If I pursue a relationship with Brooke, and at some point things fell apart, I couldn't bear to see her hurt like that."

Nathan stared at him. "You're comparing yourself to our biological father? I may not remember him, but he had a choice. A lot of choices, and every one of them defined who he was." He stared at the play yard and Mia, who had fallen asleep. "I could've walked away from Mia, but I chose to parent her to the best of my ability and to be there for her no matter what happened in the future. The situation with Gwen was a nightmare. While I can't imagine finding someone else to spend my life with right now, I have hope that the right woman will come along one day. I refuse to allow the choices Gwen made to rob me of a future."

Chess took in what Nathan said and cringed.

"That's not what I'm doing."

Nathan hiked an eyebrow. "Isn't it?"

The room had darkened as another round of storm clouds moved in over the last hour. A clap of thunder shook the apartment. Chess looked to Mia, expecting the baby to have awakened. She continued to sleep, blissfully unaware of the weather outside. "I don't know how she sleeps through that."

Nathan smiled lovingly at his daughter. "Because she innately knows, no matter what goes on out there," he pointed at the window where rain pelted the glass pane, "that I'm here for her. We can't control what happens around us, Chess, but we can control the choices we make in the midst of it all." He paused. "It's funny how everything is working out. A month ago, it was me and Mia. And now, here we are. I've gained a brother, new friends, and a new job. It goes to show, no matter how bad we think things are, the storm will eventually clear."

Thunder rumbled and even more rain plummeted to the saturated ground below. This was one of the worst thunderstorms they'd had this fall. Chess glanced at his phone and saw a tornado watch was in effect. Not unusual for this time of the year. But eventually, it would all blow over.

When the storm cleared late that evening, Chess said goodbye to his brother and niece and headed back home to Quintin. Once he was on the highway, he called Joel. A minute later, his friend's voice answered. "Hey, Chess. You okay?"

Chess thought about the question and finally nodded. "You know, I am. Better than I have been in a long time." He paused. "I'm on my way back into town. Any chance I could come by for a bit?"

"You know you can. What's going on?"

"I'd like to ask how you became a Christian. Do you mind?"

Joel's smile could be heard in his voice as he replied, "Are you kidding? I've been praying for you to do exactly that for a long time."

Chess walked into J's Parkview Diner before lunch the next day. He saw Joel near the back and waved. Joel returned the greeting with a smile. "What brings you in here? You beat the lunch rush."

He shook his head. "I'm searching for Brooke. She wasn't at work and she wasn't at her apartment. Do you have any idea where she'd be?" After praying with Joel early last night, he'd slept better than he had in a long time. His dreams had all been filled with Brooke. When he woke up, he knew exactly what he needed to do.

Anna walked up then and exchanged a glance with her husband. "She's in Dallas, looking at apartments."

Chess's eyes widened, and his heart lodged itself in his throat. "She's what? When did this happen? Why didn't you guys tell me?"

"It's not our place, man." Joel gave him a sympathetic look.

Chess knew he was right. But the thought of Brooke deciding to move on ignited panic in his chest. "Do you have any idea when she'll be back?"

Anna shook her head. "She told us she quit her job at the salon. She's planning to visit several apartments, has an interview at a bookstore, and will be back late tonight sometime."

All Chess knew was that he had to find her somehow. Still, Dallas was a big city. Locating Brooke with no idea where she'd gone was like looking for a needle in a haystack. He pulled his phone out and dialed her number, not the least bit surprised when she didn't answer.

Joel put a hand on his shoulder. "She has a two o'clock appointment at Sandover Apartments."

Chess grinned. He had plenty of time to get there before then. He waggled his eyebrows. "Thanks, guys. I've got to run."

"There are more storms on the way. Be careful!"

Chess raised a hand in acknowledgment. He jogged to his truck, jabbed the key into the ignition, and had to force himself to drive the speed limit into the city.

With the help of the GPS on his phone, he located the Sandover Apartments and realized he didn't even know what type of car she'd purchased the day before. Nerves made his palms sweaty as he closely observed every vehicle that pulled into the parking lot near the office. He wiped his hands off on his jeans for the third time as he waited for Brooke. More storm clouds moved in, and the smell of rain punctuated the breeze coming in through the partially-open window.

When he finally spotted her in a silver Corolla, Chess's heart slammed in his chest. "Okay, God. I've made a lot of mistakes. Way more than I care to count. Help me do something right for once."

He got out of his truck and jogged across the parking lot. Brooke didn't see him until he tapped on her window. Her face pale, she rolled it down and shot him an exasperated look. "You scared me to death. What are you doing here, Chess?"

"I need to talk to you." He noticed a bench, small fountain, and a variety of flowers decorating the area around the apartment complex sign. "Please."

"I have an appointment." She shuffled some papers together in the passenger seat.

He knew she was avoiding him and he didn't blame her one iota. "Brooke." She stilled but didn't look at him. "You're twenty minutes early. You're always early. Give me ten of those minutes and then I'll get in my truck and leave you alone."

She seemed to think about that and finally dropped everything she was holding into the passenger seat with a sigh. "Fine." She got out of her car and closed the door behind her. "What do you want?"

Chess put a hand on the small of her back, guided her to the bench, and sat down next to her. He took in a calming breath, willing his mind to stay clear so he could say everything he needed to say. "I'm a controlling idiot."

Brooke folded her arms across her chest and fixed her eyes on the fountain. "Yep."

He might have laughed at her response if he wasn't this nervous. "I'm thinking about selling my house."

She peeked at him from the corner of her eye in surprise. "You love that house. Why on earth would you do that?"

He put his hands on the seat of the bench, curling his fingers around the edge. "I thought I might find a place in the Dallas/Fort Worth area."

Brooke turned her head toward him, a half smile on her face. "So, you can be closer to Nathan and

Mia in Fort Worth. I'm happy for you." She returned her gaze to the fountain again, letting her hands fall to her lap.

"Except I'm not interested in moving to Fort Worth." He waited for her to say something, but she kept silent. She wasn't making this easy on him. "I thought I might move to Dallas instead."

That got her attention. She watched his face, her brows drawn together in confusion. "Why would you do that? Nathan's in Fort Worth and you've always hated Dallas."

"Well, you're moving here aren't you? Maybe I want to be closer to you."

Brooke shook her head and jumped to her feet. "This is unbelievable. You can't, Chess. I need space. I can't keep moving forward the way things are." Her voice faltered. "I've got a job interview this afternoon. I want to take art classes at the community college." She shot him a look that combined desperation with defeat. "I've got to move on. And I can't do that if I see you every day."

A drop of moisture hit Chess's cheek, and he looked up at the dark clouds above them. "I have every confidence you'll get the job you interview for. You certainly should take art classes, although with your talent, you could probably teach them." He chuckled nervously. "And I hate that everything I've done makes you feel like you need to escape from me." Another raindrop splashed on his nose.

He studied Brooke's face as she kept her eyes trained on a spot in the distance. A drop of rain hit her face, sending a smaller droplet to land on her long eyelashes. *Give me the right words here, God. Please don't tell me I've ruined one of the best things to ever happen to me.*

Brooke tried to process what Chess was telling her, but it didn't quite make sense. If he was okay with her moving on, why was he here? The falling rain increased until she lost count of the number of drops that peppered her skin.

Brooke motioned to the office. "I'm going to head in before I get soaked. Why don't you go back before this storm gets any worse?"

Chess shook his head. "I don't care about the rain."

Brooke turned toward her car, but he reached out and caught her hands in his. He tugged her gently until she rotated to face him.

He was silent until she raised her gaze to his. The unguarded emotion in his eyes took her breath away.

"You said God used me to help you and Joel. Then later to help Nathan and Mia. Do you remember that?"

She nodded slowly, unsure of where he was going with this.

"You weren't entirely right."

Now she was confused. "What are you talking about?"

"I was lost, Brooke. Back then, I was nothing but a kid who had no idea what I was supposed to do with my life. I was searching for Nathan and living in the past." A small smile lifted the corners of his mouth. "Until you and Joel came along. You two helped me to take those first few steps out of the pit I'd dug for myself." He shrugged. "Then Nathan and Mia came into my life and set me free from the guilt I'd tied to my back for years."

There was no mistaking the moisture in his eyes with the rain that was falling steadily around them. Brooke's shirt clung to her skin, and the rain traveled down her back, making her shiver.

Chess's hands moved up her arms until he was gently holding her elbows. "God might have put me in the right place at the right time to help the people who matter most to me. But last night, I realized something. God actually used you and Joel to make a difference in *my* life."

Brooke tried to grasp the meaning of his words. "What are you trying to say?"

Chess gave a nervous laugh. "I'm making a mess of this." He shook his head. "What I'm trying to say is that you were right. God never walked away from me and every time I thought I couldn't take another step forward, He sent someone to help me back on my feet. I wouldn't be where I am without you."

Brooke took in a shaky breath and let it out slowly, suddenly oblivious to the soft rain falling all around them. All she could feel was the warmth of his hands and the skittering of her heart. She moved to say something, but Chess raised his hands to her cheeks, cupping her face.

"I've made mistakes, Brooke. A lot of them. But the biggest was letting you go." He smiled, his eyes never leaving hers. "Girl, I'm so in love with you I can't think straight. You're the other half of my heart, and it took a lot longer than it should have for me to realize that."

She was certain there were more tears than raindrops on her face now. This was like a dream. A hope she'd had for longer than she cared to admit and that she'd come to accept would never come true. "You have horrible timing, you know that?"

Chess laughed. Rain water dripped from his chin and onto his already soaked shirt. "That's the story of my life, sweetheart."

Brooke chuckled and forced her face to appear serious "I'm still going to take art classes."

"Good." His thumb lightly caressed her cheek.

"And I think moving to Dallas would be a good change." One eyebrow lifted.

"I'll follow you wherever you decide to live. I'm not letting you go again."

"You promise?"

Chess grinned. "I promise. I love you, Brooke. With all my heart."

She pulled her bottom lip in between her teeth and smiled with a shake of her head. "I love you, too."

Chess leaned in and captured her lips in a kiss so gentle and loving it took Brooke's breath away. He wrapped her in his arms, protecting her from the cold and the rain, until all she felt was the warmth and love he offered.

Epilogue

"Where are we going, Chess?" Brooke kept her eyes closed tight like he'd instructed her to. It felt like they'd been driving forever.

He laughed. "You're so impatient. You'll know when we get there and I tell you that you can open your eyes."

Brooke stuck her tongue out at Chess and knew he was laughing at her, even if she couldn't see his face. The late October sun filtered through the window and warmed her skin. Her mind raced with possibilities of where Chess was taking her. He'd been cryptic since the beginning, only telling her to wear closed-toed shoes. Of all the things, it only piqued her curiosity more.

The truck finally came to a stop.

"Don't open your eyes yet." He got out of the truck and opened her door moments later, offering her a hand as he helped her to the pavement.

Brooke listened intently, hoping to catch a hint of where they might be. "How much longer do I have to keep my eyes closed?"

"You're cute. Have I ever steered you wrong?"

Brooke grinned. "Do you honestly want me to answer that?"

He planted a kiss on her cheek. "Hush. Hold onto my arm."

Chess led her through a maze of turns. At one point, she caught the scent of flowers that slowly increased until it was all she could smell. Finally, when she thought they'd be walking forever, he stopped. Gently, he guided her around and then moved his hands.

"Okay, open your eyes."

Brooke hadn't known what to expect, but the heart-shaped field of roses made her gasp. The air was filled with their scent as the white and pink blooms lifted their faces toward the sun. "Chess, this is amazing." She shook her head in wonder. "Thank you for bringing me here." She turned to smile at him. Instead of standing directly behind her like she thought he would be, he was down on one knee in the grass at her feet. Her hand flew to her mouth as tears sprang to her eyes.

Chess reached for her other hand and held it between his own. "There is nothing on this earth that would make me happier than to spend the rest of my life finding ways to surprise you. I want to keep you smiling the way you are now." He pulled a box from his pocket and opened it, revealing a ring with a small diamond and leaves etched into the band. "Brooke, will you marry me?"

A happy tear found its way down her cheek. "I want that more than anything."

"Is that a yes?" He grinned at her with that

knock-down gorgeous smile of his.

Brooke laughed through her tears. "Yes."

Chess stood and slipped the ring on her finger. He kissed her then, and Brooke melted in his arms, fully embracing a life with the man she trusted to always protect her heart.

Acknowledgments

Doug, I'm so thankful God brought us together. When I think of the chain of events that resulted in our meeting each other, it fills me with awe. You are my best friend, and I can't imagine my life without you. I love you!

This book was filled with challenges, Crystal, and I can't thank you enough for helping me work through them all. All I can say is I'm glad it finally came together. Talk about a huge sigh of relief – ha! I'm so thankful to have you for a friend and critique partner.

Franky, Vicki, Rachel, and Kris, I couldn't have finished this book without your encouragement. Thank you for your patience in reading the beginning over and over again until I finally got it right. You ladies are saints!

A big shout out to my amazing beta readers: Steph, Denny, Sandy, Doug, and Mom (Suzanne). I appreciate you all more than you will ever know.

Lord, this was one of the most difficult books I've written. So many of the scenes were emotional and came from nowhere, and I know all credit goes to You. Thank you for the opportunity to step outside my comfort zone. I pray you'll take this book and use it to bless others.

About the Author

Melanie D. Snitker has enjoyed writing fiction for as long as she can remember. She started out writing episodes of cartoon shows that she wanted to see as a child and her love of writing grew from there. She and her husband live in Texas with their two children who keep their lives full of adventure, and two dogs who add a dash of mischief to the family dynamics. In her spare time, Melanie enjoys photography, reading, crochet, baking, archery, target shooting, and hanging out with family and friends.

http://www.melaniedsnitker.com
https://twitter.com/MelanieDSnitker
https://www.facebook.com/melaniedsnitker

Subscribe to Melanie's newsletter and receive a monthly e-mail containing recipes, information about new releases, giveaways, and more! You can find a link to sign up on her website.

Books by Melanie D. Snitker

Calming the Storm
(A Marriage of Convenience)

Love's Compass Series:
Finding Peace (Book 1)
Finding Hope (Book 2)
Finding Courage (Book 3)
Finding Faith (Book 4)
Finding Joy (Book 5)

Life Unexpected Series:
Safe In His Arms (Book 1)
Someone to Trust (Book 2)

Made in the USA
Columbia, SC
16 May 2017